I0622931

IT SHALL COME TO LIGHT

M. Carolina Bento

House of Riverenza

Copyright © 2022 by M. Carolina Bento

Published in the United States of America by House of Riverenza on May 2, 2022.

All rights reserved. No part of this book may be reproduced in any form without written permission from House of Riverenza.

ISBN: 979-8-9854689-1-5

Dedicated to my family, and in honor of my sister Helena, who was a godly woman, loving mother, caring aunt, loyal friend, and a blessing in our lives.

CHAPTERS

ACKNOWLEDGMENTS

All verses from Scripture were taken from

'The Holy Bible – NKJV' (New King James Version).

ONE

I started my day reflecting on *Ecclesiastes 3*:

'To everything there is a season, a time for every purpose under heaven...
A time to be born, and a time to die;
A time to plant, and a time to pluck up what is planted;
A time to kill, and a time to heal;
A time to break down, and a time to build up;
A time to weep, and a time to laugh;
A time to mourn, and a time to dance;
A time to cast away stones, and a time to gather stones;
A time to embrace, and a time to refrain from embracing;
A time to gain, and a time to lose;
A time to keep, and a time to throw away;
A time to tear, and a time to sew;
A time to keep silence, and a time to speak;
A time to love, and a time to hate;
A time of war, and a time of peace.'

This verse always reminds us that no matter the challenges that come our way, it will be over and the opposite will reset our lives. It's true for everyone!

For me, currently, there is '*a time to stay and a time to leave.*'

I have made the decision to move away from Sycamore Place. In this lovely neighborhood my children grew up from teenagers into adulthood, and my life became surprisingly eventful in many ways.

Here I developed interests and skills that I didn't even know existed in me. As I matured and aged, my horizons expanded, and I grew into the person I was meant to be.

I was timid and quiet but as I became more approachable and opened up to others, I made many acquaintances, nurtured friendships that came and went, especially my most controversial friend, Rebekah.

It makes me nostalgic thinking that I spent a great deal of time in this place, reflecting and writing about what happened throughout my life. It's bittersweet to leave my home and a whole past behind... But I'll be carrying the memories. Unforgettable experiences!

In this perfectly manicured community of attached townhouses whose exteriors all look the same, behind the doors different people are sheltered in such close proximity, making it ironic that some neighbors hardly know each other by name.

For the first ten years of living here, I was one of them and hardly ever saw anyone outside. I was only concerned about leaving early in the morning for work, coming back in the evening in a hurry to attend to my family.

There came a time when my personal circumstances changed, and I started walking around and meeting neighbors. I realized that some older residents would not have a reason to make another choice but to stay here, while others would move away, trading the attached house for a white picket fence. Some others would go to nursing homes under the heavy weight of old age, and sadly, some have died, leaving a few widows or widowers in the neighborhood who are thinking of forming their own club.

In this place my life was transformed from being a bank assistant manager into becoming a storyteller. Who would have predicted that a middle-aged woman who never wrote anything except business reports would have the audacity to become a creative writer?

Was it accidental? Maybe not! The fact that I started paying more attention to my neighbors, getting to know the people around me, plus the desire to continue being productive, utilizing the flow of ideas running through my mind, generated an active imagination fed by my feelings and emotions, keeping me busy and fulfilling my small life.

Even brokenhearted over all the catastrophic events of the last two years, until now, have affected our country and the world, the sickness, deaths, losses of all sorts, of our liberties, jobs, financial and subsequent transformation in our way of living, I never let go of hope. And now, I am counting my blessings, feeling a new wave of optimism.

Today, I left the house for an early morning walk, and one last time, strolled around. I was melancholic reminiscing about the twenty-one years of being here, finding inspiration everywhere and in everyone.

I went to the end of the cul-de-sac and sat on a bench under my tree, its branches that looked naked and lifeless for months, now all dressed up for the spring, display the first signs of the season's revival.

A new season always brings a new beginning!

I looked up:

'Majestic, powerful tree, you should live forever.

You have been here long before us, before these houses were built around you, and you should remain long after we are all gone...

For over a century you are standing strong! Your roots, deep seated into the ground, sustained you throughout storms and blizzards, and scorching hot summers.

Under your shade I spent countless times of reflection like this,

I have learned much, I had heart to heart conversations, built friendships and trust.

Sycamore tree, my symbol of resilience and strength... Goodbye.'

I had a knot in my throat, and returned home quickly.

Everything was packed, waiting for the donation truck to come by, and our furniture was ready for the moving truck that will come tomorrow.

'What should I do today?'

With all this time on my hands this was the moment when I decided to resume writing. Lately, overwhelmed by the circumstances and my new interests I have neglected my personal project, the story of our lives that I kept very guarded, intending it to be for my children's eyes only, sometime in the future...

'I'll finish my journal today! There are so many stories waiting to be told, so many. The first one to tell is my own...'

***

I have come a long way since my early childhood in Frederick, western Maryland, where I was born and lived until the age of eighteen.

My father, Ronaldo Chaldea, was an interstate truck driver, and my mother, Janis, a devotedly religious woman, sought refuge from her daily life in prayer. She neglected my brother Ronnie and me, demonstrating she felt held back from what she liked the most, spending most of her time in church.

My mother was withdrawn most of the time, not showing much interest in what was happening with us, but she was angry about Father's long absences, due to his work.

I can honestly say Ronnie and I always looked forward to Dad being home, we had the best of times with him. He was the only one that hugged and kissed us, and said he loved us. He played with us in the park, accompanied us to school, and took us out for fun.

4

My father was very kind and caring. He would repeat he was proud of us, and was working really hard to give us both a great future!

Dad is still present in my early childhood memories as the most important figure, and for sure the most nurturing. As a little girl I adored him. Every time he would return from a road trip he would tell us stories, he always grabbed my attention.

He was humorous in the way he described other towns, cities and people he would encounter. I would never know if his stories were fictional, but I like to think that I inherited the storytelling gene from him.

Ronnie, almost four years older than me, was the spitting image of our father, not only in appearance but also mannerisms. I was the different one.

"Daddy, why are you and Ronnie brown, and I am not?"

"Because my father was white and my mother was black. I am a black man, Ellie. Your mother is white, and you have her colors, you look like a white girl, but always remember you have African American heritage, and you should be proud of it."

"Was your mother proud of you, Daddy?"

"My mother was a beautiful angel, '*Everything I am I owe to her.*' I was the one proud of being her son, that's why I named you after her, her name was Eleanora, but she was called Ellen. I see in you many qualities that she had."

"Mommy said I look like any other brunette girl, and I am not special."

"I don't think she meant it that way, Ellie, you are pretty and smart. For me you are the most special girl in the whole wide world!"

"Daddy, you are beautiful, I want to be like you."

"My precious girl. That's what you are!"

When I was eight years old Dad said he was taking me on an American history field trip to Washington, and there we went for the first time to the Lincoln Memorial, which he liked the most.

Many times before, I had heard my father speaking about his admiration and respect for President Abraham Lincoln.

Dad was proud to say that he was born in Kentucky, in the same area as Lincoln, and both left for another state with their families at the same young age. Of course they were 120 years apart, but he spoke of President Lincoln as if he had known him.

Years before he had taken Ronnie to see that monument, but he was bored on the field trip and not interested in Father's conversation. He did not want to come along this time, but Dad convinced him. He liked to have both of us together on our outings.

When we arrived at the monument, I thought it was too high to climb, too many stairs. Ronnie went ahead, running.

Holding on to my father's hand up we went, step by step, to the top.

As we looked around, Dad described it, saying it was in the form of a Greek temple, inside was a very large sculpture of Abraham Lincoln. I was mesmerized by its size and asked Dad if Lincoln was a giant.

My father was amused.

"You are right, Ellie, Lincoln was a giant in our history, but as a man he was like anyone else."

My father showed me the inscriptions on the walls, and by my request he read them out loud.

I was very impressed by the columns, the colossal sculpture, but mostly by how my father spoke, the words he used, he was enthusiastic.

I continued asking him questions.

"You'll learn everything in school, Ellie, and then you might want to come back here again, with a better understanding of this place's significance. Every time I come it brings me close to that time in our history."

Ronnie was restless, he wanted to go down again to look for a hot dog stand, but he agreed in sitting with us for a while on the top steps, looking at the long Reflecting Pool down below.

Dad mentioned that he had been there before for a march during the Civil Rights Movement, when among hundreds of thousands of people he heard the most remarkable speech by Martin Luther

King Jr., 'I have a dream…' "It was an unforgettable day!"

"Why didn't you bring Ronnie and me?"

"Oh, Ellie, that happened in 1963, he was a little boy, and you just a baby."

Father, Ronnie, and I went on with our day but he continued talking and talking about Lincoln, the places he lived growing up, and how he ended up in Washington, DC as the President.

He also referred to the Emancipation Proclamation.

Although I couldn't really understand what he was saying I looked at him in awe, and asked:

"Daddy, what is Emancipation?"

"It was when President Lincoln ended slavery in our country. The black people were enslaved. Ellie, you are going to learn all of that in school, pretty soon."

"Daddy, were you a slave?"

"No, darling, no! That happened long ago in the past, but my ancestors were, and you need to know their history."

During our ride back home Dad promised that in the near future the three of us would take a trip to every place where Lincoln had lived, to see every monument in his honor.

I was terribly excited thinking of the adventures we were going to embark on, and mesmerized by my father's knowledge. He knew many things and many places...

After a few weeks I didn't think much of what Father had told me about President Lincoln, but the impressions of that day were engraved in my memory like the words carved on the marble walls, making a mark on my future more than a young child would ever anticipate.

I don't think even my father would have imagined how that day out in DC would impact me forever. Little did I know that the foundation of my beliefs for freedom and equality starting on that beautiful day would last a lifetime.

Life went on, with Father's constant work travels, some short, others long, but when he returned he always had a story to tell about the places he saw or people he met. Dad was a people's person and made friends everywhere.

He also told my brother and me that he was planning to buy his own truck to start a local moving business, to spend more time at home with us. We were thrilled!

During his absences my mother, unsatisfied with the church she was attending, joined a new one in town whose Pastor was revered by some. She went in for a Bible study, but soon started going there daily.

She would spend more hours in the new church than at home. Even when my brother and I asked her not to leave us alone, she still would go.

My mother made no secret that being tied up at home with children was not what she wanted. On several occasions she made it clear that she never had intentions of having a second child, unfortunately I was the undesirable one…

Because of our parents' absence, for different reasons, Ronnie and I bonded, we were each other's best friend. My big brother was very protective of me, he was attentive and helped me with school projects.

Over a year later, like on any other day, my father left for one more of his interstate trips, but this time, he did not return home.

Mother shocked us telling us he had died in a horrifying road accident on I-95 North when his truck slid on the ice on a ramp, tumbled and burst into flames.

I was ten years old, and Ronnie fourteen, when we lost our father. My brother, equally shattered by the terrible loss, embraced me, and we shared our tears. We were young, we didn't know how to deal with grief. We both hurt and missed our father deeply.

Since then I relied on Ronnie more than ever. He would assure me:

"I'll take care of you, little sister!"

Mother ignored our pain, maybe she did not know what to do. She thought that forcing us to accompany her to the church's Sunday service we would forget about it… Ronnie refused, he didn't like Pastor Glenn. I had no choice but to obey her.

She was completely dependent on her religion, and very attached to the Pastor, frequenting the church that as time went on ended up being not well regarded in the community. I didn't know what was happening but there was a sort of stigma against that particular congregation.

It seemed like our mother did not miss our father, she would not talk about him, but she frequently mentioned the lack of money. 'The insurance paid by his job was not going to last…'

Throughout the following year life was sad and miserable. Joy had gone away, it felt like from then on life would never get better.

When Ronnie started high school Mother told him he needed to get a job to bring money home. Immediately he started working at a gas station after school on the evenings and weekends.

He was proud of giving all of his tips to Mother to buy us food. But, on the other hand, Ronnie was out of the house more often, and I was alone most of the time, still praying for a miracle that my Dad would return someday. I wanted to see him again, to hear his voice… As a child I had no perspective on the finality of death.

My father's absence was unbearable. I developed a self-preservation mechanism of maintaining imaginary conversations with him, keeping him alive in my mind and my heart. Many times I found myself smiling in between my tears, almost believing he was there, listening and talking to me. Those sad times lasted and lasted.

I was feeling very uneasy in the presence of the Pastor, and I did not care for his teachings. Eventually, I rebelled against my mother's demands and stopped attending the church services.

That's how we lived the next ordinary couple of years, until one October, when my brother was in his senior year in high school, another unthinkable tragedy happened.

On an early Monday morning, just two months away from his 18th birthday, Ronnie was found dead in the local park. To everyone's shock and dismay he had been killed.

The night before he had gone out after dinner, and I didn't realize until the morning, when I was getting ready for school, that my brother was not at home.

Mother crudely described the details: his hands were tied up behind his back, and his feet bound together with a rope fastened around his neck. A piece of duct tape was covering his mouth.

The Police said Ronnie died of suffocation; the rope around his neck strangled him, probably in his attempt to free himself from being bound. They were investigating, had no suspects, and couldn't find a reason for what happened. Ronnie was a well-liked boy, had no enemies and was never involved in fights.

I was profoundly devastated by the tragedy. The Police interrogated Mother and me, she had nothing to say, but I told the Officer I knew my brother had friends and he was going to meet them, but he did not mention their names.

The Officer looked through his belongings to see if there were any clues, nothing was found.

The pain of losing my brother in that manner was excruciating and just exacerbated the pain of losing my father years before. I wanted to die, I wanted all to be over, to be with my father and my brother.

I prayed, 'Dad, take good care of Ronnie and take me away.'

I cried endlessly throughout months, until I realized I had to keep living. I wanted to make my Dad proud, to show him I was strong. I was the only one to tell his story, and to continue believing in the things he believed and taught me.

My mother gave me her old Bible.

"I only go by Pastor Glenn's teachings, I don't need this. But you might find something in here that will make you stop crying. Some people do."

I was fourteen years old, I had no interest in reading it, but I kept it until one day I started looking through the pages. It was difficult to understand but in the back of the book I found a reference verse finder, from then on I read a few inspiring passages, trying to find solace in my loneliness and in the never-ending grief for my father and my brother.

> *'Blessed are those who mourn, for they shall be comforted.'*
> Matthew 5:4

That became a habit, and as time went on I developed a liking for the psalms, some sounded like poetry, and I started believing that I was not alone anymore, and my heart would be healed.

> *'The Lord is my shepherd; I shall not want. He makes me to lie down in green pastures; He leads me beside the still waters. He restores my soul.'*
> Psalm 23:1-3

Much later on in my life I realized that my mother had given me the best she had, and I became grateful to her for that.

Nevertheless, I was frustrated with her for not doing anything, not talking or pressuring the Police for an answer on Ronnie's death. She kept repeating, 'It was God's will.'

I clearly knew that was not God's will, it was an act of evil, a heinous crime that could not go unpunished. For me, my brother's life was worth the world!

At that point Mother gave me some more bad news, we had to move out of our house, a modest but comfortable home on Gary Lane, the first house I called home, into a little two room shack behind the church's building and part of the Pastor's parsonage. It was an awful place, cold and unfinished. She explained the Pastor had offered it in exchange for her services to the church.

From then on, more than ever, Mother would spend all of her time with him. Pastor Glenn lived alone, he had a wife when he settled in Frederick but she had gone away.

That happened during my first year of high school. It was isolating and depressing. I was known as 'the murdered boy's sister,' the other students didn't want anything to do with me, but I continued going to school and in my alone time I would browse through the Bible, trying to understand and accept my life's reality.

I knew that like most of the other students I was not going away to college, I would need to start working to support myself. I couldn't count on anyone's help.

In my junior year, around President's Day, our history teacher organized a field trip to Washington, DC to visit some monuments.

The school bus parked at the side of the Lincoln Memorial. As the students started looking around and going up the steps, I became emotional and clearly remembered the day when I was eight years old when Father took my brother and me to that same place.

As I arrived at the 'Temple' and stood in front of the majestic and solemn statue, I started reading the words engraved on the back wall out loud, like my Dad once did:

"In this Temple as in the hearts of the people for whom he saved the union the memory of Abraham Lincoln is enshrined forever."

My classmate Kayla, basically the only girl who talked to me, approached me. I had tears in my eyes.

"Why are you crying, Ellen?"

I couldn't respond and ran back to the steps, sat alone against a column and sobbed. I didn't know where all of those tears were coming from, the emotions I was feeling were very powerful.

Other people were looking at me with curiosity. Kayla went to get the teacher that was chaperoning.

Ms. Myrthes came to my side and kindly asked me:

"What's the matter, Ellen?"

"I just remembered, I was here with my Dad and my brother when I was eight years old, the three of us, it was a great day. Dad spoke so much about President Lincoln, he had great admiration for him. Right now I am feeling horrible that I am here alone, they are gone, and I want to remember every single word my Dad said that day... I need to remember, I am the only one left to tell his story."

I continued sobbing, Ms. Myrthes put her arm around my shoulders.

"I am sorry you lost your father and your brother, I am truly sorry, Ellen. You will remember, spend as much time as you want here, you don't have to walk around with us anywhere else. But, stay inside, it's too cold out."

Kayla volunteered to stay with me.

We went back into the chamber and sat together until I dried my tears, and I looked at the walls, south and north.

"My Dad read this out loud for me, right now I can hear his voice reciting his favorite quote from Lincoln's Gettysburg speech:

'I leave you, hoping that the lamp of liberty will burn in your bosoms until there shall no longer be a doubt that all men are created free and equal.'

"It was a memorable day, Dad told me he brought me here because he wanted me to understand what this monument symbolized to him.

He said he had a book about Lincoln that he carefully read and treasured, and it was available to me when I would learn about this President. I need to ask my mother if she kept it.

He continued talking about how Lincoln was the most courageous and good hearted President in history!

I remember everything now. He also referred to the 'I Have a Dream' speech by Dr. Martin Luther King Jr."

I thanked Kayla for being a good friend, and later we reunited with our classmates in the school bus to return to our hometown.

Arriving at home I asked my mother for my father's book. Fortunately, she had kept it with a few of his belongings and gave it to me.

For the next days I started reading Lincoln's biography, which gave me an idea.

The students were assigned a project to write an essay about our field trip to DC. Instead, inspired by the first years of Lincoln's life, I chose to write a fictional story about two little boys – Ron, the son of a servant, and Abe, the son of the master of the land, who growing up together became best friends, and by age eight, moved with their families from Kentucky to Indiana.

The imaginary experiences they had together since their first steps, the companionship and joy the two little boys shared, their achievements and also their sorrows, first of moving away from their birthplace, and then in Indiana, where they both lost their mothers to a plague.

Both boys cried together, and they formed a bond unlike any other that kept them united until the end of their lives...

Ms. Myrthes was touched.

"This account of Lincoln's childhood is unique and heartwarming, it was written with love. Ellen, you are talented, you might go into writing someday. Beautiful work!"

How important are the words of a teacher! Because of Ms. Myrthes I started believing in myself, that I was able and capable of doing something special. I never forgot her...

After that memorable field trip Kayla and I got closer. For months as I was making an effort to read the biography, tedious at parts, others eventful and riveting, I shared some with her.

It was wonderful to have a friend with whom I could share my thoughts and interests.

Learning more and more about Lincoln as a man, a father, a President, something exceptional happened... I poured out the pain that was locked in my heart, I experienced a sense of healing, thinking of my father I identified similarities in both of them. I felt lighter, releasing much love that I had contained in my heart for my father and admiration for his wisdom.

I told Kayla:

"Only a great man can see greatness in another! My Dad was a great man, and I thank God, Ronnie is with him..."

"Ellen, I understand how much you hurt for losing your Dad and then your brother. Regarding your brother, there is something that bothers me, and I keep thinking about it. I was made to swear I would never tell, but we are friends and I would like to help you..."

"What are you talking about, Kayla?"

"Please, just don't get me involved in it, my family is very scared. It's about my cousin Marla, she was your brother's classmate and they were friends, but Marla had a boyfriend, Troy, who was very jealous and didn't want her talking to anyone else.

14

I heard that one day he set your brother up, making Ronnie believe that Marla was waiting for him, instead Troy and his friend Rusty showed up to teach him 'a lesson.'

When Marla heard the news about Ronnie's death she suspected and confronted Troy, who threatened that if she ever said anything she and her family were going to pay for it."

"Kayla, what you are saying is so serious. Are you sure? Where and when did you hear that?"

"At home, my Mom and Marla's mother are sisters. My aunt was telling my Mom that was the reason Marla went to college in Philadelphia, to be far away from Troy, who killed Ronnie because he didn't like him, he was different."

"Who was different? My brother? Was that because he was biracial?"

"I am not sure what she meant, that's all I heard. My Mom made me swear that I would forget about it... They are still very scared that Troy would hurt Marla."

"Do you know the guys' full names?"

"No, the only one I know is Marla's of course. But I swear she is a good person, she didn't do anything wrong, she was just scared for her life."

"Does Troy still live around here? What about Rusty? Was he a participant?"

"No one ever said anything about seeing Troy around, but Rusty works in a car repair shop on Main Street, they say he is a good guy. Promise me, Ellen, please don't involve me, my Mom and my Aunt would never forgive me."

"Thank you, Kayla, I promise you I won't involve you in this, but something needs to be done. My brother was murdered, he deserves justice!"

My heart was pounding fast, as soon as I arrived at home I told my mother and asked her to go to the Police with that information.

"Mom, they are not going to pay attention, I am not even seventeen yet! But they will listen to you."

To my surprise, my mother refused.

"You need to forget all about the past, Ellen, everything happens for a reason. It was God's will!"

"Mom, I am really mad at you now, God does not want young boys to be killed, my brother, your son was murdered! Why wouldn't you do anything about it?"

"It might be all gossip, Ellen, don't listen to it."

I never felt so irate in my young life, I was very angry at my mother for her neglect and excuses for not doing what was right, for her blind trust in that pastor, she was becoming weaker, he was brainwashing her...

I thought for a day, didn't say a word to anyone, not even to Kayla, and after school I went to the Police Station looking for an Officer. As soon as I identified myself as Ronnie's sister they directed me to Detective Hitch.

I proceeded telling him what I had learned from 'some people' in high school, and asked him, begged him, to investigate.

He kindly told me the case was still open, they believed that they were eventually going to close in, and urged me not to comment with anyone about my visit to the Police Station 'to protect myself.'

A month went by, I didn't hear anything until Kayla told me:

"Something is going on, Marla told my Aunt that a Detective from Maryland went to see her to ask her questions about Troy. She was scared, but she told him she did not know where he is, and she told the truth about his threats to her family and herself.

It looks like they have a lead in your brother's case."

"I hope they do, Kayla, I need to have that peace, my brother will be vindicated."

I called the Detective, he told me things were moving right along, he had Rusty cooperating with them. They were looking for Troy, who had moved out of state years before, and his family claimed they had no idea where he was...

It took another couple of months, when one afternoon Detective Hitch showed up at the coffee shop where I was working after school.

"Troy is in custody! He was living with some relatives in

Alabama. We have him back to be arraigned, he will go to trial."

My heart sank.

"Thank you, Detective Hitch. Thank you! What about Rusty?"

"Rusty was a witness to the crime, not an accomplice, he was also lured to that encounter not knowing of Troy's intentions. He is cooperating fully with us, and helped us dig up the information we needed to find Troy, he is also testifying against his former friend."

I told my mother of what was going on, but she did not demonstrate any interest. How could she be that cold?

Justice had come for my brother, he was being vindicated, but for me it was hollow, nothing would ever bring him back. I loved him, I missed him, but it was time to let go of the sorrow. I cried, it had been four years since he was gone. Ronnie...

That evening I lit up a candle and said a prayer for his everlasting peace in the arms of our Father, in heaven.

> *'Finally, brethren, whatever things are true, whatever things are noble, whatever things are just, whatever things are pure, whatever things are lovely, whatever things are of good report, if there is any virtue and there is anything praiseworthy – meditate on these things.'*
> *Philippians 4:8*

Right at the beginning of my senior year I was experiencing a mix of peace and anxiety... Peace for having the deep belief that my father and brother were together, and anxiety about my future.

I dared to dream I would go to the community college, and with a part time job I would be able to support myself. Even living in very poor conditions for so long because we couldn't afford anything better, I hoped my mother would agree.

I told her about my plan, but she surprised me once again.

"I have some news for you, Ellen. Pastor Glenn, a couple of parishioners and I are going to a spiritual retreat in Arizona over the summer. It is part of his investiture. So, as soon as you graduate you need to move out of here."

"Why? Can I just stay until you come back from Arizona?"

"It might take a while, I don't know… We might settle there."

"Mom, lately I have heard rumors about your Pastor, people in the neighborhood say that he is a fake and runs a cult. Is that why you are going away with him?"

"That's not true, Pastor Glenn is a god! I will follow him anywhere he goes."

My heart was broken.

"What about me, Mom, where do I go?"

"I thought you should go to Baltimore, you'll have more opportunities there. I already called my cousin Gayle who lives in Timonium, you know her. I asked her to let you be there with her and her family until you find a job and a place to live."

I was devastated and scared.

"Mom, you have lost your mind, you are able to leave your only daughter for the Pastor! I think he is creepy. He is no god, he is evil."

That evening I thought how my brother was my age when he lost his life, now my own mother was leaving me… No matter what, I had a life to live, but why, why did I have to do it alone?

I read inspirational words over and over, but did not find any comfort. The world was a scary and sad place.

'The Lord is near to those who have a broken heart, and saves such as have a contrite spirit.'
Psalm 34:18

The last few months in Frederick were devastating. I was crushed and had to make an effort not to hate my mother, that insensitive, fanatical woman who didn't know how to love her own child. I needed her, I wanted her to say she was going to stay with me, and working together, I could go to college. With time I would have to work on myself to try to understand and forgive her.

I never missed my father more than those days… If he and my brother were there, they would never have abandoned me.

My friend Kayla said that if she were to remain in town she would invite me to live with her, but she was excited about going to the university in Pittsburgh, just a couple of hours away from our city. I was losing my only friend too. We said goodbye.

I had no prom, no graduation party, no family.

Against my will I had to leave my hometown, it was painful and I vowed never to return, not even to visit the cemetery. I would carry and honor my father and brother in my heart, for as long as I lived...

On the eve of my eighteenth birthday, I gathered the little I had, a few pieces of clothes, my two favorite books, my old worn out Bible and Lincoln's biography, the most precious gift from my father. I never parted from those books, I still have them in a drawer in my nightstand, I often hold them and read some passages, they have been with me throughout everything!

When the day came, my mother accompanied me to the train station, she told me she would write to me at her cousin's address.

At the last minute I asked her:

"Mom, do you have any doubts you won't ever regret what you are doing?"

She looked anguished and confused, and did not respond.

I wanted her to hug me and tell me she loved me and she was not letting me go... But I was stoic, so was she, stoic or plain insensitive.

She only said:

"Have a nice trip to Baltimore, Ellen. I know you are going to be just fine, you have guts, more than I do."

There were no hugs or kisses. Like a mean teenager I told her:

"Really, Mother? I want you to know that when I was little I wanted to be just like my father, kind, smart, loving, and I still do. I will miss him and honor him every day of my life."

That was my way of saying I would not miss her.

I boarded the train, wishing I would not regret being that mean to her.

The train took off to Baltimore.

I was shaking in fear of the unknown ahead of me.

I prayed:

'Preserve me, O God, for in You I put my trust.'
Psalm 16:1

During the trip, I hoped that my mother would come to her senses, would leave the Pastor, and that she would call me back home or maybe join me to start a new life, the two of us, mother and daughter, as it should be.

TWO

My cousin Gayle was kind enough to pick me up at the Baltimore station with her daughter Denise, who was two years older than me. I had seen them only twice before in Frederick, the last time was at my brother's funeral.

Gayle brought me to her small and crowded house in Timonium. She was older than my mother and had three grown children, Denise and two sons. One was away in the military, I never met him. Her older son slept in the basement all day and was out all night, he was a bouncer in a night club. Occasionally he would disappear for days, and when back at home he looked grumpy. He never spoke to me.

She showed me a room that I was going to share with her daughter.

Denise didn't warm up to me, she mentioned many times she was not pleased sharing her room. She made me feel like an intruder.

Gayle made sure that I knew the arrangement was temporary

and it was not free, I had to pay for food and use of utilities.

I needed to find a job immediately. She had it all worked out and directed me to go immediately to the local supermarket just blocks away from her house. 'They are always hiring.'

I got a job, didn't pay much, but Gayle was happy. She could count on the extra income every two weeks when I paid her.

Once I overheard her talking to Denise, asking her to be patient with me, because I was paying for all of their food bills and more…

Sometimes I was irritated by Denise constantly giving me advice on how to dress and use makeup, which I didn't. She was working at a makeup counter in a department store. She was good at it, but a little too much for my taste.

Denise was also hardly home, going out often with her friends. She never invited me to come along anywhere.

For the first two months I was anxiously waiting to hear from my mother.

Gayle had a conversation with me. She called my attention to the fact I was always reading at night, staying late in the living room with a light on, and that was increasing the power bill.

"What are you reading, Ellen? The Bible? I am afraid you are going to be just like your mother."

"I am not like my mother, I am more like my father was. Yes, I do like to read the Bible, a verse or a psalm at times, it comforts me."

"Sorry, I really don't think you are like Janis, you are normal, she was more like a 'church roach,' a fanatic."

"Fanatic, that's true! Was my mother always like that? How was she before she was married?"

"She was weird. She was raised very strictly, my uncle, her father, was a nut job. Her mother had no backbone and didn't help Janis develop her personality. My side of the family knew she was troubled. Something is still wrong with her, I couldn't understand why she was going to Arizona with her Pastor. She totally lost her mind this time!"

"That's what I sometimes think, my mother has a mental issue. Her devotion for that Pastor is irrational. I fear she doesn't realize what she is doing. I worry about her, I wish I could help her."

"No, Ellen, you can't, and it's not your place, you are her child, she should be with you. You have been here for months and not a word from her... Unfortunately, I agree, Janis has a mental condition. You don't know the whole story..."

"What is it, Gayle?"

"Janis was never a girl like the others, and when she was fourteen she attempted suicide. It was ugly and bloody, she cut her wrists. She was saved, of course, but coming out of the hospital they recommended long term rehabilitation. Her parents put her in a home for troubled adolescent girls, run by nuns, where she remained for a couple of years.

When she came out she was another person, like a robot, quiet, always had a rosary in her hands, praying constantly. That was the time when I got married and came to Baltimore. Years later I went back to attend Janis' wedding, and I was very surprised.

I don't know how a girl like her married someone like your father. They were so different!"

"Yes, my father was gregarious, kind, loving. He did love us, my brother and I... He was gone too soon. And I am sorry I never knew of my mother's struggles, it might have been hard on my father."

"Well, didn't you know, Ellen? You mother was always dependent on her church Pastors, if they would not give her special attention she would leave."

"I remember when I was a child and she went to Pastor Glenn's church. My father was still with us, then."

"I know, but it did happen once before when she had left for a while and returned home months later, your father took her back. I don't know how to say this, you were born soon after she returned. My family was certain that Ronaldo was not your true father..."

"How can you say that, Gayle? He was my father, my real Dad, he loved me, I loved him."

"I am sorry, Ellen, I know he was an exceptional father, I didn't mean to offend you, but didn't you ever question why you look nothing like him or Ronnie?"

That conversation hurt me deeply and made me angry. I thought Gayle was cruel. I wanted to forget what I heard.

My Dad was and would always be the one that I loved and admired the most.

The ugly truth was I never felt loved by my mother. She had made clear I was the undesirable child, 'with nothing special about me.' I would never ask her about what Gayle told me, but I was motivated to look for her.

I called the church in Frederick, the phone had been disconnected. I then called a neighbor who confirmed my mother had left with the Pastor the day after I had moved out or maybe that same day, she was not sure.

Although I was uncomfortable in Gayle's house, I stayed, hoping that I would hear from my mother soon.

I worked at the grocery store as much as I could and accepted all the overtime offered to make more money. I had ambitions to go back to school, but after I paid for room and board almost nothing was left.

That's when I remembered that Lincoln was self-educated. He only attended school intermittently from ages ten to sixteen. He was an avid reader and nurtured an interest in learning while working all sorts of odd jobs. However, it was said that he didn't like hard labor, he preferred to write and read constantly.

When he was living in Illinois, working first as a postmaster, and then a county surveyor, he decided to teach himself to be a lawyer, studying English law and other law publications. He stated: *'All I have learned, I learned from books.'*

He was admitted to the Illinois bar and began to practice law in Springfield, before he became an astute politician, which led him to be one of the best Presidents of our country. For me, he will always be the best!

'If Lincoln could do it, I can do it! He will be my mentor! I do not have to remain ignorant for not being able to afford school. Where there is a will there is a way!'

That day I felt my Dad would be proud of me. That was one of the lessons that he left me when he passed on his admiration for Lincoln to me!

I did some soul searching…

'What do I want to learn? Business? History? Literature?'

I went to a used bookstore in our area to look around, it was overwhelming, books of all sorts, on shelves, in piles on the floor. I had no idea of what to get until my eyes fell upon an entire collection of Charles Dickens, beautiful books in a red leather cover with a gold trim, for only $60.00! My heart stopped.

In high school we had worked on 'A Tale of Two Cities,' I would have loved to read it again, and all the other ones, but I only had $4.00 and some change with me. I went to the cashier, an old gentleman, and asked him:

"Sir, I really, really would love to have that Dickens collection, but I can't afford to buy it right now, I only have $4.00. But, I can sign a note and come by every payday. Please, I really need those books."

He looked at me and laughed.

"That's not how I do business, young lady, why do you 'need' those books?"

"I love literature, I want to read every word, every book, I want to be educated and know all the beautiful words of the English language."

"I see, but you only have $4.00."

"Do you think you could hold them for me? I'll save more, I'll work overtime."

"What's your name? Where do you work?"

"I'm Ellen, I work at the supermarket as a cashier, but I won't be there forever, I plan to upgrade my job."

"You will, you are ambitious, Ellen. Let's make a deal. I'll save the collection for you, and every time you come you'll take a book for $2.00 each. Today you can take the first two. I made that special price for the collection, expecting to sell it at once, but I trust you'll come back."

"Thank you very much, Mr..."

"My name is Hardy."

"Thank you, Mr. Hardy, are you sure you won't sell the other books to anyone else?"

"No one else, they are yours, I'll just be keeping them, but don't take too long, I'm old, you know..."

He asked me to bring all the books and placed them behind the counter. I paid for two.

"What other books do you like to read, Ellen?"

"I just have an old Bible and a biography of Abraham Lincoln that my Dad gave me."

"You like Lincoln! I have tons of books on him."

As I was leaving, Mr. Hardy gave me a little book of Lincoln's quotes.

My heart melted.

That day I arrived at Gayle's house with my 'new' books and started reading them with much enthusiasm, they were the best thing I had ever owned.

In my prayers that evening I thanked my Dad for teaching all he knew. I missed my father and my brother like they were gone just yesterday...

By the time my nineteenth birthday came around I had my entire Dickens collection. Mr. Hardy honored our deal and became my 'new' old friend.

I would go to his store often just to talk to him and browse. He was like a grandfather figure and showed interest in my future employment plans, suggesting that I take night classes for professional advancement.

He also recommended other classic American authors like Louisa May Alcott, Ralph Waldo Emerson, Henry David Thoreau, and gladly I started forming my own little collection.

During that time I received a most expected letter from my mother, but I was disappointed it had minimal information and no return address, postmarked from the city of Tucson.

She said she had committed to the group settling in Arizona for good as one of Pastor Glenn's wives, and did not say if she would come back someday.

'Wives?' I was shocked! I had the feeling that she would never return to Maryland. Our lives had taken different directions. In other words she let go of me, permanently...

I was hurt, but not surprised, I had witnessed my mother's blind faith and trust in that man, he was her crutch, she was extremely dependent on him and impaired of good judgment.

Her last decision only confirmed what I suspected; my mother was mentally incapable, but I was still disappointed.

When I realized for certain she would not be back, I had no reason to wait in Gayle's house for her. I had been there for a year, it was time to move on.

Cousin Gayle reminded me, more often than not, that my situation was temporary. She made clear she was helping me out of pity, and the extra income was helping her, it worked both ways. But, Denise was always cranky about the room, making me feel unwelcomed sharing that space.

I was looking forward to find my own place. I also wanted to progress professionally, and started wondering what kind of job I would search for, maybe in a fancy department store!

Every time I walked across the street from the supermarket to a bank to cash my meager paycheck and interacted with the friendly tellers, I thought it was an upgrade, I could do that job.

I asked a teller if it was difficult to get a job like hers. She gave me an application and directed me to an office to speak to the human resources representative.

It was easy! I was employed by that bank but in another location far from there, in Baltimore County.

I told the supervisor that trained me for the job that all the money I was making was going to pay for room and board, and I couldn't afford even to think to go to college to advance the possibilities of a career.

The supervisor told me of the training opportunities that the bank offered, I could and should pursue them. She also suggested that I move closer to their location to save money and time in transportation.

One thing led to another, and someone told me about a lady who rented rooms in her house, in that neighborhood.

I met Mrs. Crosby, an arrangement was made, and I moved out of cousin Gayle's and went to my new 'boarding house' to a small room of my own.

I maintained contact with Gayle, hoping that someday she would receive news from my mother… That never happened.

Still the salary was low enough that I couldn't afford anything else, only basic needs, food, a few work clothes. I became an expert in finding professional outfits in thrift shops, which I did for years.

During the first two years at the bank I attended all the training courses related to my new job and developed a very good reputation, making fast straits to become a senior teller. That's when I qualified to get classes at the local community college for professional advancement, paid by my employer, which led me to a new position as a customer service representative.

I had my own desk, attending to customers with information about the bank's products, opening new accounts, et cetera.

I was proud of myself. I would think of my father. 'Can you see me now, Dad? I am moving forward.'

I dealt with all sorts of customers, electricians or contractors who would come in their work overalls, lawyers and businessmen in gray suits and ties.

That's when I noticed a customer who looked different from the others, he had been coming to the bank more often than not, always wearing a leather bomber jacket and Ray Ban glasses, like an old fashioned pilot! He was charming, nodded and smiled at me.

Until one day he approached my desk and introduced himself:

"I am Craig Froy."

He asked me questions about obtaining a home equity mortgage. He told me he had inherited a house from his grandparents in the neighborhood, and had decided to renovate it to eventually sell it.

He showed me some drawings of his plans for the house. He also told me that he had lived there most of his life, but many years before he had moved into an apartment near the airport, to be close to his work.

I asked him if he was a pilot.

"No, I am an air traffic controller."

"That might be a very interesting job."

"Indeed, it's very involved."

I gave him the information he asked for, and told him I needed some documentation for an application.

He came back a couple of days later, and I directed him first to go to the County Office to record the Deed in his name. I explained the legal ramifications of it, without that we couldn't proceed. He thought I was an expert.

"Aren't you too young to do this job?"

"No, I am twenty-three, I have been with the bank for almost four years, now!"

"Are you in college, Ellen?"

"No, but I have been taking some courses in finance and customer service at the community college."

He returned, and his loan was immediately approved.

Craig was happy and said:

"We need to celebrate! What about if I come by the end of the day and take you out for dinner?"

I wanted to accept it, but there were rules.

"Sorry, Craig, but I can't do dinner with customers."

"What about lunch, a business lunch?"

"That will be alright."

"OK, I'm off on Thursday. At what time may I come?"

"I'm out at 12:30."

Two days went by, and I became anxious to see him.

Craig was waiting for me outside the bank.

"There is a nice Thai restaurant right around the corner. Do you like Thai food, Ellen?"

"I never had Thai food, but I would like to try it."

We had a pleasant time, I loved the coconut shrimp he ordered. We didn't talk about 'bank business.' He was the most mature, interesting man that I had been close to. Craig was in his thirties, independent, and had a profound commitment and passion for his job.

"Ellen, that thing you said, you can't go out for dinner with customers... What about your personal life? Are you allowed to go out on your time, with whomever you want? Or is there someone in your life?"

"That's not it, there is no one, but I don't mix my personal and professional lives, that would be unethical."

"I see, let me make myself clear, I am interested in getting to know you better. Would you like to go out with me?"

I couldn't say no.

"But you can't come to meet me at the bank."

"Fair enough, give me your phone number and address, I'll pick you up at your house."

I was sorry I needed to interrupt him to return to work. He walked with me back to the office.

We went on our first date on a Saturday night.

Craig was the first man that showed personal interest in me. That was the day when I stopped thinking of myself as just an 'ordinary girl.'

He wanted to know everything about me. I gave him a short description of my family, and the lack of it.

He spoke very little about himself and mentioned he was raised by his grandparents.

"Grandparents from which side, maternal or paternal?"

"They were my mother's parents."

"Was she there, with you, with them? What about your father?"

"No, she was not there. She left me with her parents and took off. They told me she came to see me a few times when I was very young. I don't remember. I never met my father. That's all."

It was obvious he was very uncomfortable talking about his family.

We continued seeing each other regularly. I enjoyed his company.

With Craig I felt special, just like in childhood when my father told me I was special. Craig told me I was bright and beautiful, and he was with me for the long run. He said that was unusual for him, before meeting me he did not want to be connected to anyone.

I fell in love with him. He was my first serious boyfriend and the only love of my life. His love and attention made me feel accepted, worthy, made me whole.

But there was one subject that he didn't talk about, his family.

I could see he had been hurt as a child, was it because of his mother's rejection? His father's absence? I would never know.

I went with him through all the process of his house renovation, he asked my opinion about finishes and colors, and was always proud of showing me the progress.

He became very enthusiastic about the project and ended up doing much more than initially planned. With that he decided he was not going to sell the house for a profit.

After one year into our relationship he asked me to move in with him.

"As you see the house is perfect, and I decided I would like to live here. What about if you move in with me, Ellen?"

I thought for a little while. I would love to live in that beautiful house with him, but I said no.

"Craig, I can't take a risk and live with someone like that, I am alone and want to build a family of my own, and have a home…"

"In that case, why don't we just get married?"

And that was it, no romantic words, no big gesture of getting on his knee and asking me, no diamond ring.

"Married? Oh, Craig, I love you, I'll marry you."

"I love you too, Ellen, you'll make the perfect wife."

Craig didn't give me a wedding party or honeymoon, but he bought me a car. My first car, a used maroon VW Beatle, 'to make my life easier.' It did! He was not romantic but was thoughtful.

I bestowed on him all my love and attention, and we embarked on a life that felt very promising.

At the age of twenty-five I became a mother, our daughter Suzanna, Suzy, was born, and my life took a totally new meaning. I wished I could stop working to take care of our baby, but I couldn't, we had a home loan to pay.

Craig was responsible in supporting our family, but it was not enough for everything we needed. He continued being very dedicated to his work and spending long hours at the airport, including holidays and weekends…

Emotionally, he was not available or understanding of my needs, and he didn't know how to be patient with a small child. He left the care of our daughter entirely up to me.

I was lucky finding proper day care in our neighborhood, splitting myself between my job and the family.

Motherhood was an incredibly fulfilling and challenging time, my heart was full of love for my baby, and obviously I had less time to 'pamper' Craig.

After I had my daughter I realized that my mother had left a hole in my heart. 'How could a mother forget her own child?'

I wondered about her, I never heard from her again. Occasionally, I would contact Gayle, she never received any letters either. I needed to know what had happened to my mother. Was she alright?

I decided to try to find her, I called for information and wrote a few letters to authorities in Tucson, Arizona, relating that my mother had moved to that area seven years before. I gave them a few details I had on her and her Pastor, and waited.

Many weeks later an answer came from the City's Sheriff Office stating they didn't have any records about either one of them in Tucson or the surrounding areas, he went further and checked the system for the state of Arizona. To make it more puzzling there were no records that they had ever settled in the State or had obtained a driver's license there.

The Sheriff informed me that there were some religious groups or cult communities close by that did not allow any outside interaction.

That was the end of any hope that I could have in finding my mother.

I had no hard feelings, and I continued praying she would be well, hoping that maybe someday I would hear from her...

I dedicated myself entirely to my daughter, amazed by the wonderful baby she was. The most beautiful baby, with green eyes and reddish hair! She could only resemble Craig's family, I asked if he had a picture of his mother, he didn't, and did not 'remember' how she looked... Hard to believe!

Craig didn't want to talk about his mother, only once he remarked his grandparents were ashamed of her lifestyle, without explaining it.

Two years later, I was pregnant again, it was not planned. Craig was not supportive, he did not want any more children. Despite his opposition I welcomed the news and immediately made arrangements with the day care where Suzy was so well taken care of.

It was privately owned by a mother and daughter. For many years while I worked I relied on them, and I will always remember how caring and thoughtful they were.

Another surprise happened on Christmas Day, our little boy was born, four weeks before the due date. As he was a Christmas gift, I called him Nicholas! I was very upset because Nicky was born a little underweight and had to remain in the hospital for ten days.

Because my newborn son needed some special care, I was able to arrange an extension of my maternity leave and stayed home with my daughter and son until he was three months old. Although challenging it was a glorious time. I wish it could have been always like that.

Nurturing and loving my babies healed my heart, and I became the mother I wish I had...

My days were taken by much work, I felt in many ways depleted like a single mother, but I couldn't complain. Craig was there, but with an obvious dismissive demeanor that made me feel not supported or loved. He did not respond to my efforts to make time for the two of us, to talk to plan for our family, to deepen our relationship. In consequence the romance between us faded away, and he would say that was just like married life should be, all about work, responsibilities and providing for the family.

As the children were growing up, there were very few occasions when we had family time that was fulfilling, and he praised me, 'Our children have the best mother' but he wouldn't say 'I love you.'

Over the years he continued displaying his emotional detachment from the children, and I would invite him to talk things out, just to be put off, 'Get used to it, that's the way I am,' he would say.

Was that because of the manner in which he was raised? Definitely! He was not willing to discuss his upbringing, only mentioned that his grandparents had given him what he needed, a roof over his head and education, but he always felt like he was a burden to them. They didn't love him.

My husband was a responsible, honest man, but sadly, emotionally broken, unable to express his feelings, to give or receive affection.

I had made a mistake when initially I believed that both of us being denied love and affection in our early life would bond us further. For my part I was committed to give all my love, to nurture our relationship, and I thought he was too...

I was broken-hearted facing the reality of a loveless marriage.

'And this too shall pass...'

Suzy and Nicky were growing up beautifully, two adorable, loving children. Suzy was brilliant and funny, since a young age very articulate.

Nicky was a sensitive and smart little boy, gentle mannered, very attached to me and dependent on his sister. He reminded me of my brother.

'Behold, children are a heritage from the Lord; the fruit of the womb is a reward.'
Psalm 127:3

Throughout their childhood I told them stories of my father, and of course of Abraham Lincoln, and made up tales of the adventures of two little boys, best friends 'Ron and Abe.'

The children delighted in the stories, and I would get enthralled with them, I wished I had time to write them, but life was too busy then...

The three of us would do everything together: outings, movies, beach in the summer, visiting museums and monuments. As Craig was not available, my fun experiences were all with my children, I hardly socialized, my friends were mostly work friends that I would see from Monday to Friday at the office.

I continued working at the same bank, supervising a large clientele of all sorts of customers, commercial and personal, and was promoted to a branch assistant manager.

I settled in the job. I had holidays and weekends all dedicated to my family, and the money I earned was to provide for the children. I was determined that both my daughter and son would pursue their education goals. I was working to support them.

At home, alone at night, after the children were asleep, I would feel lonely... Craig's coldness seared my soul.

I didn't live the life of a woman, a true wife, I was just a mother, a housekeeper.

I couldn't share my beliefs with Craig, he had no interest in listening, but I held on to them. I didn't profess any religion but gave my children a Christian education, without imposing it, I wanted them to follow their own path when adults.

Here and there I would mention a psalm, a verse, words of faith, of acceptance and love, for them to be familiar with the things that sustained me spiritually.

Sixteen years of marriage went by fast.

It looked like things would always be the same, but surprisingly when Craig was fifty-three years old, all of a sudden he had a grin on his face. He was offered a position at a major international airport in Virginia!

"Let's move to Virginia! It's a great opportunity, we will have a very nice home after selling this house."

He was enthusiastic, I saw the possibility of a better life for all of us, the children never had seen their father so motivated, I couldn't take that opportunity away from him, and hoped that it would turn things around.

I told Craig I would move for him and for our family, believing that it was for the improvement of our relationship.

I was ready to quit my job, the local bank didn't have representation in Northern Virginia, I would find new employment there.

Craig was thankful.

"I know it is a sacrifice for you to leave the bank after so many years, you won't regret it, Ellen, you might not even need to work full time anymore, we'll have more time together, a bigger house, and great schools for the children."

I was hopeful that was our turning point!

Suzy was starting high school and agreed with the move, but she cried a little as she would have to leave her elementary school friends behind. Nicky was fine, he was starting in a new middle school anyway.

We went together to explore Northern Virginia and liked it.

The area we chose to move to, Sycamore Place, impressed us.

It was a quiet and elegant community on a wide street off a busy road, splitting into two shorter ones converging into a common area partially surrounded by nature, which was very pleasant.

There was a small, well-kept garden, a mini playground for the few children that lived in the community, and a couple of garden benches for residents to relax.

The most striking thing about that place was that right behind it there was the most amazing and colossal old tree, standing strong.

The classic attached houses with brick facades, looking all the same, were built on both sides of the streets.

Our children didn't mind the tiny yard, now they were teens and didn't miss having a yard to play in. And another good reason to live there was that the schools in that area were excellent, offering special programs.

The house was more expensive than the one we had in Maryland, but Craig wanted to give our family a nicer home. It was a little distant from the airport but he didn't mind the commute. As a matter of fact, he enjoyed the long drive. He seemed happy with this change in his life.

I was optimistic and hopeful, believing this was a turn for the better for our family.

'For I have learned in whatever state I am, to be content.'
Philippians 4:11

THREE

As we settled in the new neighborhood I observed that was one of those places where nothing exceptional happened. The residents knew each other in passing, they were cordial, they collected newspapers from others' front doors or driveways when they were away, like in any other place in America where good citizenship prevailed.

Some of the residents had a dog, and that's when they met and greeted the neighbors while walking their pets, which were treated like a family member.

All sorts of people lived in those houses, but predominantly an older population of retired singles or couples. Younger couples usually wouldn't stay long, they would move out when they had a child or two, into suburban houses with yards and white picket fences.

We had one of those in Maryland, where our children grew up…

As planned I was looking to work at least until the children finished college free of debt. I found a full-time position at a local bank but took a step down working again as a personal banker, building a new clientele.

The four of us had a good start. Craig was more open to talk and spend time with us, he even invited us twice for family outings but as soon as the children resumed school, life went back to what it was before.

Craig, being his old self, was enthusiastically working long hours, totally immersed in his new responsibilities, spending much more time at the airport than at home.

Again, I was lonely at home, enjoying every bit of the company of my children, participating in school events, and when they were available we would engage in some leisure activity, like visiting museums and monuments in Washington, DC.

Suzy and Nicky adapted easily to the new schools. Suzy, the social butterfly that she was, made new friends quickly. Nicky continued being the same quiet and reserved boy.

When Nicky started high school, to his father's disappointment, he did not join any sports, he preferred to be part of the chess and drama clubs!

Nicholas, as he asked me to call him in front of others, was artistic, he liked theater and had talent in producing and also wanted to be in plays, which eventually he did, very successfully.

Getting closer to her graduation Suzy had a conversation with me, she decided to apply for colleges close to home. I was happy I wouldn't lose her companionship.

"You have me, Mommy, and you still have Nicky living at home for a little while longer…"

At that time Nicky was sixteen years old, I was concerned about my son's timid demeanor. I spoke to him about high school friends, girls, bullies… For the first time I told him what had happened to my brother.

My children knew I had a brother who died very young, but they didn't know the tragic circumstances.

Nicky was shocked, my intent was for my son to be aware of emotional situations or out of control feelings, like jealousy, envy.

"If anyone would ever bully you or threaten you, don't shy away, tell me, tell the school authorities, protect yourself, son."

"Mom, you worry too much, nothing will ever happen to me. I'll never get involved in a situation like that..."

Suzy, being a wonderful sister, was empathetic:

"Mom, I am sorry for your brother, I imagine how much you hurt. I am really sorry."

Two years later when it came time for Nicky to apply for college he told me he didn't want to stay close to home like Suzy did. He wanted to create some distance to establish his own independence.

My son told me he loved me, and we would always be close, but he had been in conflict for a while not telling me the truth, he was afraid I would reject him. Bluntly, he said:

"Mom, I am gay!"

I was confused and perplexed.

"But, Nicholas! Are you sure?"

"I am, I know you are not judgmental, Mom, but you have religious principles, how do you feel about this?"

"I don't know how to feel, Nicholas, is this just a phase? I think I am scared that people would misjudge you, give you a hard time, or opportunities would be taken away from you..."

"No, Mom, this is who I am and I can't change it. For years I lived in conflict, having feelings that were taking me in another direction. You see, I never had a girlfriend in school, only friends, they are mostly girls. I know I am disappointing you, and for that I am sorry."

"Are you sure? You are only eighteen, you haven't had enough life experience yet! How come I didn't see this coming? Was I oblivious? Did I pay enough attention to you, Nicholas?"

"Mom, you are not responsible. This is who I am."

"Did you meet other gay boys in high school? Did you have any relationships?"

"There are other guys, we are friends, I never had a relationship with anyone."

"Son, thank you for confiding in me, but I need to be completely honest with you, I do not understand the gay lifestyle, in many ways I think it could be the result of a physical dysfunction or a hormonal issue... If that is the case, maybe it could be treated.

On the other hand, I know there are people that have sexual dysfunctions, or are morally deviated, as the result of abuse, you were never exposed to situations like that!

This issue goes against my beliefs and principles. Nicky, I am worried, you are too young, please reflect, and if there is anything I can do to help, just tell me. Don't ever forget that no matter what I love you."

"Don't worry, Mom, things have changed, this is much more common than you think, I will be alright. I don't mean to upset you, I don't doubt you love me, that's why I count on you."

"I just want the best for you, son, but please be careful, be cautious of whom you associate with. Protect yourself from disappointment and hurt. And if you need any support, I am here for you always."

I embraced my son and cried, I was concerned. I didn't tell him but there was some disappointment thinking that Nicholas, my sensitive, delicate son, would face hardships just for being himself. I was also afraid of his father's reaction.

"Are you going to tell Dad about it?"

"I think I have to, Dad never had much time for me... Sometimes I think he always knew I was 'different,' that's why we never bonded."

"I don't think so, your father is emotionally detached, as you see, he never bonded with any of us, his feelings are all for his career, he is passionate about it."

"More than passionate, Mom, he is obsessed! But, I will tell him about myself, I just want to ask you to be there with me. I don't want to get into a fight with him."

That evening I hardly could sleep. I remembered my brother who had an identical demeanor as Nicky, and I heard rumors in high school that 'Ronnie was different.' Was that what they meant? I would never know, but I felt guilty, maybe there was a gene on my side of the family, and it was passed on to my son…

I prayed for my son and continued hoping that he would be true to himself, and not influenced by societal trends.

On a Sunday afternoon, after Craig returned from his leisure trip to the airport and sat to read a newspaper, Nicholas approached his father and told him he was going away to Virginia Tech, and about his sexuality…

Craig exploded in surprise and anger, he didn't know how to restrain himself from using offensive words. I interfered and asked him to calm down and just listen to Nicholas. He didn't, he stormed out, blaming me for what was happening.

"It's all your fault, Ellen, you raised him like a girl! You still call him Nicky!"

Nicholas stood up for himself and me.

"I am the way I am supposed to be, Dad, there is a genetic component, a chromosome, and that is all. Do not blame Mom for it, that's unfair."

Craig stormed out of the house. I embraced my son.

"Don't be upset, Nicholas, he will turn around."

"As far as I know he won't, but I'll be OK without his support, I have been so far with just your love, Mom. By the way, you can call me 'Nicky' as much as you like!"

Craig did not attend our son's graduation or bring him to college.

Suzy and I drove to Blacksburg to bring Nicholas to his university. I cried many tears leaving my 'little boy,' now a handsome young man.

He told me:

"It'll always be like old times when we were little, the three of us, even apart we are together."

On the way back I told my daughter:

"Suzy, just thinking the house is going to be emptier, I'm so glad you are still with me."

Little did I know that same year Suzy found an internship at a publishing company in Silver Spring, Maryland, and tearfully told me she needed to live close to work, the commute would take many hours of her day away…

"But I will come to see you often, Mommy."

She was excited, anticipating that the internship would lead to a job, and eventually she would go for a master's and I would not have to worry about helping her financially anymore. She thought I was doing enough for her and Nicholas.

I helped my daughter find an apartment to share with a roommate, in a very nice and safe building, and I continued helping her financially until she was able to afford it on her own.

I had less time with my daughter, but our closeness and friendship was never broken.

It was extremely lonely for me, being home without my children, I was not used to coming home to an empty house, and I started working more than ever. With Suzy still in college, and four more years of tuition to go for Nicholas, I had to continue going, doing it all alone…

Suzy graduated with honors. I was so proud of her! It was also my achievement, I've accomplished what I set myself to do.

Upon graduating Suzy was offered a permanent position at the publishing company. She was absolutely happy about it.

A few months later she told me:

"Now that I am working with an Editor in Chief I see so many things that are not worthy of being published, and I think you have a talent, Mom, put it to use. Remember when we were little the stories that you told us about 'Ron and Abe'? Why don't you write them in your spare time?"

"Suzy, who, me? I'm just a banker, I like to make up stories, but writing them?"

"Yes, Mom, you know more than you give yourself credit for. Write, write, you might just have found a new hobby that will keep your mind busy, and you'll bring joy and also positive information to children, like you did to us."

"I'll think about it, Suzy, and thank you for the compliment. Only you could say something flattering about me."

42

I continued working to maintain Nicholas in school. He was doing very well, enthusiastic about his courses, and very involved with the drama club.

My husband was completely withdrawn and avoided any conversation about our son. But, I never missed an opportunity of approaching him and asking to talk about ourselves, our children. He continued evading.

The fact that I was clearly supporting our son put a larger rift between us. I sadly believed it was the end of any hope I still nurtured to have our relationship fulfilled...

Craig was stubborn, in my heart I knew he would never concede.

Sometimes after work I would go for a walk alone around my neighborhood to visit the small garden area, and weather permitting I would sit under the tree shade in contemplation of its magnificence.

I observed that the residents were friendly, but until then only saying hello and smiling, we hardly knew each other. That changed.

A neighbor, walking his dog, introduced himself:

"Hi, I am Phil, I live in 4332. I have seen you around this tree."

"Nice meeting you, Phil, I am Ellen, I'm in 4360. Lately, I have walked around this area after I come from work, if it is not too late.

I was admiring this tree, it's gigantic, but it is so old, the bark is peeling off..."

"No, it is just the way it is, this is a sycamore tree, and it's easily distinguished from other trees by its mottled bark flaking off."

"Oh, that's what it is! I never saw one of these before."

"You don't see many of these in this area, we are lucky to have one here, these large specimens are located mostly in the Shenandoah Valley.

Sycamore trees grow for over one hundred years to massive proportions, reaching up to one hundred thirty feet high, and up to thirteen feet in diameter."

"Thank you, Phil, for teaching me that. Over a century old! It's a lasting example of resilience throughout time. It's obvious why our community is called Sycamore Place! I have lived in this neighborhood for nine years and until now I have spent very little time enjoying and learning about this impressive tree."

From that day on, I had a 'friend' in the neighborhood and I started paying more attention to the people around, and introducing myself when I had the chance.

On another occasion I saw the neighbor across the street, an old lady standing on her deck while chimes were ringing in the wind in beautiful sounds... I stopped at the side of her house, and addressed her:
"Hi, I am Ellen, I was listening to your chimes, it sounds whimsical..."
"Nice meeting you, I am Grace. Thank you, they remind me of the sound of my homeland."
"Where is your homeland?"
"Korea, South Korea."
Grace was married to an American man who sat in a wheelchair.

Whenever I would see Grace outside I'd wave at her and ask her how she was doing. She always smiled, a sweet smile, and would say nostalgically, "I am still here."

I felt a need to connect to people, to know more about them. I couldn't bear the silence and emptiness in my house, I needed to fill that space with something, even if it were just with my imagination.
I also met Gloria and Dario, a retired old couple that always walked holding hands. They were so cute! They looked like the perfect companions. I imagined they had traveled through life united together for decades!
Sometime later in one of our brief encounters on the sidewalk, Gloria told me they would be moving away, to be close to their daughter, who was also alone after her children had grown and moved out.

One afternoon, coming back from my favorite place, Phil was

coming up the block, pulling his dog strongly away from someone's front yard.

"If I let him go the homeowner would be watching from behind her shades. She is crazy!"

"I never saw anyone here, who is she?"

"I don't know her name. She is weird, she doesn't like people. I heard she only comes out in the midnight hours to care for her flowers, or to sit on her deck, my friend that lives next door once saw her outside in the middle of night, he said she looked ghostly, her skin was almost transparent!"

"Well, it might have been the moonlight… Anyway her flowers are beautiful!"

Needless to say that at this point I knew that Phil was the neighborhood 'busybody,' he always had something to say, and it was not always positive. But, I was intrigued.

'A lonely woman who doesn't like people and comes outside only in the middle of the night. Maybe she needs someone to talk to, or maybe she suffered some trauma…' I was curious, I would like to meet her, someday.

Suzy came home for the weekend, if I didn't have my daughter I would be also a lonely woman. Together we went to visit Nicky on Saturday, I missed my son very much. Sometimes, I wouldn't see him for months.

On a warm night the following week, I was not sleepy and impulsively thought of going for a walk in the direction of the lonely woman's house. I never did anything like that before but the will of seeing that person was compelling. 'How deeply lonely she should be, alone in that house, coming outside during the late hours under the moonlight! If she is so reclusive, why would she choose to live in this kind of community?'

I questioned my sanity, 'What am I thinking?' I couldn't control my thoughts, I felt compassion for someone who I knew nothing about. 'Maybe she needs help.'

From then on every time I walked in front of her house I would stop briefly to admire her flowers, hoping that she would be behind the curtains, and I would wave, like she could see me, and maybe someday she would come out to talk…

It happened one gray late afternoon… I stopped and waved when I noticed the large front window curtains were pulled to the side, and I could see the silhouette of a woman, with her hand up, waving back at me.

I was startled, smiled at her and made a sign that I liked her flowers. I don't know if she understood me, but we made contact!

I was standing on the sidewalk, perplexed. I wished I could introduce myself and tell her, 'Your daisies are beautiful, you take good care of them, they are my favorite flowers.'

I went back home as fast as possible. I felt awful realizing how profoundly lonely I was, any opportunity that I had I wanted to connect with other people.

My children were not there every day, they didn't need me anymore, Craig and I hardly had anything in common…

A couple of days later I saw Phil around, and as always he had something to say, but he would not talk about himself, until I asked:

"Why doesn't your wife walk with you, Phil? I never saw her except sitting on your deck."

"Lena has a heart condition, and to make things worse, she suffers from anxiety, she has panic attacks."

"Oh, I see, it might be devastating."

"I take care of everything she needs, my wife is not like that 'Lady of the Night' that has everything delivered to her front door, and no one ever sees when she picks up. She is really weird.

Mostly recently my friend has seen her late in the day, standing by the front window staring outside, no one has seen her face, her windows are tainted. Crazy!"

"Well, Phil, people suffer from different ailments, maybe she has a medical condition. Have some compassion!"

I didn't continue the conversation, but 'the Lady of the Night' was still on my mind… I saw her shadow at the window a few more times, and like before she waved back at me.

Weeks later, Phil couldn't wait to tell me 'that woman' was

gone. He was told that two nights before a dark unmarked van came to her door and took 'a person' in a stretcher. It was not a first responder's vehicle. In the morning a moving truck came and took the house furnishings.

I felt sorry for her. I didn't even know her name, in my mind I called her Daisy. Pretty soon her flowers dried out…

During the next two years Nicky would come home only on his vacations, Suzy and I occasionally went to Blacksburg to visit him.

Craig continued working almost every day, even on his days off he would go to the airport, and many times he worked the most diverse hours, nights, days, weekends, holidays. Like he always did, he was not slowing down, and his time in our house was limited.

Finally, Nicholas' graduation came! I was thrilled thinking that he would stay home for the summer searching for a job, or maybe he would decide to continue in school for a master's, but instead he had found a job with a government contractor in Washington, DC, where he was moving to be on his own.

At least DC was so much closer to us… I sighed.

"Mom, you helped too much, now I am responsible for myself and my bills, you should retire and take better care of yourself. You look tired."

I was really tired then, I didn't tell my son and daughter I was facing a troublesome period at work.

Due to a financial crisis many small banks were closing or merging with larger corporations, and massive layoffs were happening.

The situation with my bank was about to be decided. My fellow workers and I were on the brink of losing our jobs.

With that added stress I was feeling exhausted and strange symptoms arose. I consulted a doctor who told me I had chronic fatigue syndrome and was deficient in Vitamin D and B-12, he prescribed high doses, recommending extensive periods of rest.

I took the vitamins, tried to rest as much as I could but it didn't minimize the symptoms. I was frustrated.

Suzy at that time had a new boyfriend, Blake, and things were going well for her. She also suggested I retire.

"Stop working, Mom, stay home, you are young and have a lot ahead, take care of yourself and write, just write!"

"Well, I might one of these days, I am on the brink of being laid off."

"Things happen for a reason, Mom, you need to rest and then you might use your time to write those stories you told us when we were young, we couldn't wait for the next and the next."

"Funny you say that, Suzy, I have been reading about Lincoln lately, his life story still fascinates me but I forgot those childhood stories, they were improvised.

When I was in high school I wrote a paper on Lincoln's childhood that gave me an enormous satisfaction and awards from my teacher. I don't have that paper anymore, lost in time… Maybe I'll write another one based on the same idea, in more detail. All I need is time to do it! Thank you, Suzy, for motivating me."

One afternoon when I was returning from work I saw a nursing home van taking away Grace's husband, behind it there was a truck with their belongings.

Grace was standing at the sidewalk, she was teary, ready to board the van, she looked at me in a very sad manner:

"I am going away. I can't take care of the house and my husband anymore… I'll miss you, lovely neighbor."

I blew her a kiss. "You'll be missed, Grace. May God bless you and your husband. Have a peaceful life in your new home."

After I saw Grace leaving, I thought I hadn't been a good neighbor, she lived across the street from me and I hardly knew anything about her. I was intrigued learning about her country, South Korea.

That evening I spent hours researching. Before going to bed I looked through my window, her house was dark and silent, there would be no whimsical sounds of Grace's homeland again…

After a few weeks there was some movement, the house was being remodeled, someone new was going to move in.

Days later, one afternoon when I was returning home, there was a moving truck in front of the house. I got out of my car and saw a mature couple, the man went inside the house, the woman was on the sidewalk, and immediately came in my direction.

I greeted her, "Welcome to the neighborhood!"

She introduced herself, Rebekah.

"Nice meeting you, Rebekah. I am Ellen. I'm here in case you need any information about this area."

"I sure will, Ellen. I'll be talking to you."

"Have a nice moving day, Rebekah. See you later."

She was pleasant, looked refined, I had a good impression.

On the next weekend, during my morning stroll, Rebekah came outside.

"Mind if I join you?"

"Not at all, Rebekah, I enjoy the company."

"I'm spending too much time in the house, I have been thinking of getting a dog, everybody has a dog around here. Do you know of any shelters in this area?"

"I don't have a dog, but there is a shelter in the next town. If you want something specific there is also a kennel not far from here. My neighbor Phil, a few doors down to the right, got the cutest puppy there. He can give you that address."

"Is Phil friendly? Sorry to say, people around here are so quiet. You are the only one that greeted me."

"I agree, it is a quiet neighborhood, but they are nice. Phil likes to talk, he is out every day with his dog."

"I'll ask him. It was nice seeing you today, Ellen, I suppose you work, but whenever you have time I like talking to you."

"Me too, Rebekah, I might have more time soon, I am facing a lay off."

"Sorry to hear that, these are hard times, maybe it will be for the best. It's good to take a pause and direct our attention to ourselves sometimes."

Suzy and Nicky surprised me with a special celebration on my birthday, the 50th! I didn't want a party, I was not feeling well, but went along anyway.

Right after it I fell ill, the occasional mild symptoms such as fatigue, numbness and tingling in the legs, dizziness, and blurred vision that I was trying to disguise took a sudden turn for the worse, and I had mobility problems, I couldn't hide it anymore, literally I couldn't walk.

That day I stayed in the downstairs den that we used as an office, and when Craig arrived home later he found me in a debilitating state. Immediately, he took me to an emergency room and called our daughter.

I never had been seriously ill. After days in the hospital and many tests I had the devastating diagnosis: multiple sclerosis!

I knew nothing about that disease. The doctors explained it was an autoimmune disorder affecting the central nervous system, spinal cord, and it was not curable and not possible to predict its progress, it varied from patient to patient.

There were treatments available that could effectively slow down the disease, reducing the number or severity of relapses, but that would take time. However, they diagnosed my case as the most common form of MS involving episodes of new symptoms followed by periods of remission, during which the symptoms could go away.

Anyway, I was impaired of working for a long time, and the doctors recommended I apply for disability.

My children were at my side, holding me up, motivating me.

"Mom, you have so much faith, you are going to be alright, we'll do anything to help you through this."

I was feeling sick, fatigued, practically disabled, and had a long road ahead but was determined to recover from that nightmare.

'*This shall pass...*'

Craig was initially attentive, he provided medical care, had the downstairs room set up for me, agreed with a nurse coming to give me injections, and a physical therapist as needed, and he even was more communicative with Suzy and Nicky when they came to see me.

Suzy took time off to spend two weeks at home to help me. She said the new neighbor from across the street had asked about me.

"She hasn't seen you in a while… I think you should talk to her, Mom, she looks very friendly. It is nice to have a friend around. Also Phil, he is a talker, asked me how are you doing, I told both of them you were in the hospital but you are recovering well."

"Suzy, please do not mention the MS to anyone. I am fighting it back, it will go in remission, I am praying for that.

Anyway my doctor told me that I should consider disability and not return to work. I wouldn't return, we were all just laid off and I am going to be impaired of driving for a while…"

A week later my daughter was driving me to a doctor's appointment, with her help and a walker I was slowly approaching her car, when Rebekah came to greet me.

"Hi, Ellen, I met your daughter the other day and asked about you. I don't mean to intrude, but did you have hip or knee surgery? Are you feeling better?"

"No surgery, Rebekah, it was something else, and yes, I am much better, on my way to a full recovery, thank you!"

"Ellen, I am a retired nurse! If there is anything I can do to help, I'll be glad to, here is my phone number, please call me, I'll be right over."

"Thank you, Rebekah, I'll keep you in mind."

I told Suzy I found Rebekah a pleasant woman, I was looking forward to see her again, maybe we would become friends.

"I need friends."

"I think she does too, Mom."

My appointment went well, I was becoming more independent again, but I would need to continue with physical therapy for a while.

I insisted for my daughter to return to her life and her work. Suzy continued coming to see me often.

Nicholas had concerns, he asked me how Craig was treating me.

"He has been fine, he checks on me every day, takes care of the bills, hired a cleaning woman. In a way he surprised me, I am grateful!"

"I am glad my father has a heart after all."

"What about you, son, how are you doing? How is your life in DC? You can tell me anything, you know it, don't you?"

"I know, Mom. Everything is fine, my job is great, they are very pleased I created a new computer program, and I have new friends. Let me ask you, Mom, how would you feel if I have a boyfriend?"

"Nicky, be careful who you bring into your life, I never want to see you hurt."

Truthfully, I never took lightly the idea of my son being gay, I accepted who he was but I was in conflict between my faith and beliefs and my love for him. I believed it was challenging for him, I just wanted Nicky to be happy and kept praying that he would live a fulfilled, authentic life.

Rebekah came to my door.

"I am on my way to the supermarket, do you need anything, Ellen?"

"Thank you, Rebekah, as a matter of fact I do, I need some fresh fruit."

"Listen, when I come back, I can spend some time with you practicing your exercises, would you like that?"

"You are kind but I do not want to impose, Rebekah, you have your commitments and your husband..."

"I do, but what you don't know, Ellen, is that I spend much time alone, which is not good, makes my head spin. My husband spends a lot of time in his office in DC, sometimes he stays overnight."

From that day on Rebekah insisted on having time scheduled with me, to help me out with my exercises. Our time together was productive, and that marked the start of our friendship. Pretty soon my therapist released me from the sessions, all I needed was to keep moving and practicing the skills she had taught me.

As I improved, Craig return to his old self, he was cordial but not really interested in knowing how I was feeling physically or emotionally. He would come home and would stay around me just for a few minutes, then would go to his room 'to work' as he said. I wouldn't see him anymore until the next day when he was going or coming...

But I had my children's attention, also the care of my new friend. Looking back I never had a friend like Rebekah. I had only acquaintances and two 'work friends' with whom I maintained phone contact after we were laid off from the bank.

The next time she came around, Rebekah showed me her new puppy.

"Ellen, this is Goldie, my golden retriever, that is the dog of my preference, this breed is kind, friendly, trustworthy, intelligent, I can go on and on... My family always had golden retrievers when I was growing up, I love them."

"She is adorable!"

"Pretty soon you are going to be able to come for a walk with me and Goldie."

"I feel hopeful and stronger, Rebekah. I pray for that, and I am determined to walk on my own again without the assistance of a walker or leaning on anyone."

"You will, Ellen, I am sure you will."

'I sought the Lord, and He heard me, and delivered me from all my fears.'
Psalm 34:4

I saw my hours of loneliness as an opportunity to place my entire attention into researching and writing by hand a new project that I was determined to complete, and produced considerable work in just a few weeks.

During that time I was transported to another place, another time, and didn't feel the aches and pains of being ill. That was therapeutic!

I showed my work first to my daughter.

"This is a work of love, Suzy. I went back to the past when I wrote an essay about Lincoln's childhood, and also the fictional short stories about the two little boys Ron and Abe that I told to you and Nicky, when you were little.

This is a lifetime portrait of friendship and loyalty, although there are some real references and timelines, it is not political at all."

"Mom, that's fantastic! Please, tell me from the start."

I began...

"The owner of the Sinking Spring Farm in Kentucky was an anti-slavery advocate. Although he had bought two of his workers, he treated them as his employees, providing them with independent log cabins, free Sundays for rest, and a small pay for their services.

In the year of 1809, two boys were born; Abe, the son of the master of the land, and Ron, son of the worker's family.

They were raised together, and from the time they started walking, Ron and Abe were inseparable. Many of those early adventures you already heard in your childhood.

When Ron and Abe were eight years old their families moved to Indiana, and settled at the Little Pigeon Creek Community.

Initially, their boyhood was full of fun, learning and laughter, but in September 1818 some of the residents came down with a plague named 'milk sickness' that took many lives, including their mothers.

Abe was very attached to his mother, whom he later referred to as an angel.

'All that I am or hope to be, I owe to my angel mother.'

United in pain the boys formed a deeper bond, and as they grew up they had much more in common.

Ron, the strong, handsome young black man, became his supporter and confidant, and remained at Abe's side as his helper for everything.

They were supposed to work together, clearing land, plowing fields or building fences, but often times Ron worked the hardest while his friend would sit under a tree with a book in hand.

In that place Abe, the tall, young white man, read books that opened his mind, and he flourished intellectually.

'I do the very best I know how, the very best I can, and I mean to keep on doing so until the end.'

In Indiana Abe solidified his position against slavery, the same sentiment that he had learned from his father:

54

'Those who deny freedom to others, deserve it not for themselves.'
'As I would not be a slave, so I would not be a master. This expresses my idea of democracy.'

In 1830 they moved to Illinois. Abe became a lawyer, a leader in the community, and started his political career counting on the firm support of his most loyal admirer and friend Ron, who during that time acted more like an assistant, a bodyguard, protecting his friend from everyone and everything.

They continued spending time together, discussing issues of all sorts. Ron was not formally educated but he was bright, had common sense and insights that Abe appreciated. As he ascended in his political career Ron was standing by him all the way, as his personal friend and advisor.

Through victories and defeats they remained together. Nothing would demote them. Ron's steady support with his words of encouragement and strength, and his good humor were a balm to Abe's most adverse and challenging times. He wrote:

'To ease another's heartache is to forget one's own.'
'In this sad world of ours, sorrow comes to all: and, to the young, it comes with bitterest agony, because it takes them unawares.'

Finally in 1860, Abe was elected President of the United States. Ron couldn't be prouder!

In 1863, after a long debate and war, Abe ended slavery, protecting escaped slaves. After signing the Proclamation, Ron humbly kissed his friend's hands:
'Thank you, my courageous brother, for saving my brothers.'

In Washington, to remain at his friend's side, Ron took a humble position as the footman and coachman. Whether in the White House, or out driving the President's carriage to events, they were always together.

In all occasions Ron was his anchor, laughing with him or crying with him, through all the glories and all the pains that Abe suffered. Through power, conflicts, anguish, losses there was Ron, the most loyal of friends.

The last time Ron drove his friend out of the White House was on April 14, 1865, to Ford's Theater. He didn't know that was the last time he saw his best friend alive...

Their friendship lasted for their lifetime, just to end so tragically.

Ron died shortly after of a broken heart..."

"Oh, Mom, this is touching!"

"Suzy, this fictional tale is inspired in part by real facts. It was emotional to write about Lincoln, for me the most fascinating person in American history, and also about my father. On these pages Ron, my Dad, is immortalized forever as the hardworking, loving and loyal man he was. I gave him a long life besides his hero! As a daughter I did what I was supposed to do.

Reading about Lincoln as an adult it gave me more inspiration, he too didn't have much formal education, he was self-educated and look how far he went, and what he did! I admire him even more, and I like to believe that both my Dad and Lincoln met in heaven. 'Ron and Abe together forever.'"

"Mom, I appreciate you so much, I am proud of you. You are my *angel mother*!"

"It's nice to hear those words, my father used to say it about his mother, he learned from what Lincoln wrote about his own mother..."

Suzy told me she was taking my manual script to type it and edit. But I did want to do it myself. She kindly offered to get me a new computer with a bigger screen, to make my work easier. The old one I had was obsolete.

FOUR

I was on my own again. Craig stopped paying attention to me, he would come and go, many times going straight upstairs without talking to me. That was disheartening but consistent with his behavior before I got ill.

However, this time was different... My children were grown, they were sensitive, and if I needed I could count on them. I considered myself lucky.

In the midst of it all I had a new friend that was collaborating with me more than anyone ever had. I was grateful for Rebekah's friendship, it came at a very significant time. I did let her know of that.

I had lost a friend recently, my ex-manager Gordon died of a sudden heart attack, possibly caused by the heartache of losing his job after thirty years. He was devastated after the layoff.

I also heard from Iris, my co-worker, she was just diagnosed with lung cancer, I felt terribly sorry. So sad... My old time friends were departing.

Suzy came home on the weekend and brought a proof copy of my book. I was emotional when I held it in my hands. That was the biggest reward I could ever dream of.

The birth of my first book! My intent had been to leave in writing a story about the people that I loved and admired, to the two people that I love the most, my daughter and my son.

"I can't believe it, Suzy, you did this for me. I am so happy."

"You did it, Mom, thank you for making me a part of it, I am your editor and manager. We should have our own business."

"Business? I didn't think of that, I am just having fun, and in the process I found a way of fulfilling my time, not losing my brain capacity.

It's hard when we stop working, first goes the daily mental stimulation, second we lose our social community, friends... But, just look, Suzy, I also have news for you!"

With the help of a cane, I walked to the foyer and went up the steps to the main floor.

"Mom, this is fantastic! Be careful, please, don't lose your balance."

"I won't, I'm being careful. The first time I did this, Rebekah was here and she spotted me."

"She has been a great friend."

"She has, but I only agreed to her helping me once a week, I really don't want her giving me so much of her time. But it is always good, she has great conversation, she is optimistic. I truly enjoy her company."

After a long period indoors, I was ready to start walking outside again. It was a nice sunny day in the fall, a pleasant temperature. I stood on the driveway alone, I was a little shaky, afraid of falling, but determined to go for a walk in the direction of the garden.

Rebekah joined me, holding Goldie.

We reached the garden area, and I looked at 'my tree' for the first time in months. I missed it! I almost wanted to speak to that living, majestic tree that I was also a survivor of a storm. 'We are still standing!'

"So, Ellen, I see you like the sycamore tree! I do like it too, there were many where I grew up."

"Where did you grow up, Rebekah?"

"In South Carolina, in a remote, rural and poor area north of Lake Marion surrounded by a forest."

"That's interesting, it would be very hard to guess that you came from a rural area, you are so elegant, well spoken..."

"I learned those skills after I left that place and went to school, I left all behind but never forgot I grew up very poor. To feed our family my father would hunt wild ducks or turkeys, that's when the retrievers helped collect the birds. That's the reason I got Goldie, my family always had golden retrievers, I loved them..."

Rebekah showed some emotion.

"You became emotional remembering your childhood, your family... Would you like to talk about them?"

"Ellen, now that you are moving around we can get together for coffee in my house, I'd love to tell you where I came from."

It seemed like a long outing, I was tired and returned home. I told Rebekah, if she had the time the next day, we could get together to talk. I had something to tell her, that it was not health related.

"What is it, Ellen? I am curious."

"I'll tell you tomorrow... Thank you for coming with me on my first morning walk after so long."

"Ellen, I also have something to share with you tomorrow."

During our next visit I learned about Rebekah's childhood:

She was the third of seven children, four girls and three boys. All of them had biblical names: Aaron, Ruth, Adam, Rachel, Abigail and Timothy.

In Rebekah's early memories her mother, a devoted woman, was always pregnant, therefore extremely busy, taking care of the children, the vegetable garden, sewing their clothes, and having very little time to nurture each of them individually, and herself.

The two youngsters, Abigail and Timothy, had a large difference in age from the first ones. Her mother was depressed, she had a series of miscarriages and a stillborn in between the older children and the two younger ones.

Her father did some odds and ends, cleaning yards, cutting wood to warm others' places to be able to feed his family. He would work on whatever was available, and he would spend long periods away from his family, mostly during the crop season or planting. There was very little time left for the children.

At age fourteen, Rebekah decided she was going to continue in school, and against her father's advice she started attending Lake Ethel High School, at the same time she did some babysitting jobs in town to supply her needs.

Since she met the school nurse Rebekah thought that was the best job she could ever aspire to, becoming a nurse was her dream.

Her two older siblings, Aaron and Ruth, were already married, and it was her father's desire that Rebekah would be married as well, soon. He discouraged her of her dreams, telling his daughter she had no means to relocate to their capital or Charleston to attend school. For their family that was impossible to accomplish.

But she did it! Upon graduating from high school, she was accepted to an accelerated nursing school program in Charleston.

"It's amazing, you did it, Rebekah!"

"Someday I will tell you more about how that happened, Ellen!"

"You have so many brothers and sisters, aren't you in touch with them?"

"No, over the years I went back only a few times to see them. It was very sad, mostly to attend a funeral... My parents died before they reached sixty. My two older siblings even before that, then I lost my sister Rachel during childbirth. There were only two remaining, the youngsters Abigail and Timothy, they both married at age seventeen and nineteen like all the others and moved away... We lost contact."

"That is so sad, Rebekah, your entire family was gone soon!"

"That's what poverty does. Lack of medical care, bad nutrition, any complication with an infection or a flu would easily kill. They had children, they were spread all over with other relatives, the older ones were on their own..."

"It's tragic, I am sorry. I know what you mean. I also grew up in poverty. But that is a story for another time."

"It was painful. I always felt I was by myself, with no family. I only had my son, Patrick..."

That day Rebekah showed me some pictures she had on the shelves.

"This is my son when he was younger, this one is more recent, with his children. Patrick is now forty, he is the light of my life."

"He is very handsome, Rebekah. Do you see him often?"

"No. He has a full life with his wife and her family in Atlanta, he is very close to them. But I visit him as often as I can."

"He is far but at least you can see him. I know the heartache of being away from your children."

"Let's not talk about sad family stories, Ellen. I want to show you these pictures hanging on the stairwell wall, I painted them."

"You are an artist, Rebekah. They are beautiful!"

"That's what I do for a hobby or entertainment when I am alone..."

"That's amazing! I came to tell you that I wrote a book, my daughter Suzy is publishing it! Can you believe it?"

"Oh my goodness! That's what you have being doing? That's incredible, Ellen. You are a writer!"

"I don't think of myself as a writer, I just wrote a story that has been in my mind for a long time. Suzy incentivized me to do it, I had so much fun and joy with it that I am thinking of a new story already."

"Look at us, we have an artistic vein in common, you write, I paint, that's bonding, isn't it, friend?"

"I think it is!"

Suzy and Nicky called me every day and came on weekends to see me. Sometimes Suzy would return to Silver Spring to be with her boyfriend, but Nicky would stay with me for the whole weekend.

Their companionship always meant the most to me.

I told my daughter that during the last month I created a new story, totally different from what I had written prior.

"What is it all about, Mom?"

"I was inspired by the old couple that lived in Rebekah's house before she moved in. Do you remember them?"

"I remember seeing the lady a few times, what was her name?"

"Grace, I spoke to her once about the chimes she had on her deck. She told me she was from South Korea. I had seen her husband sitting outside in the driveway, he was American, I think he lived in the downstairs room, he couldn't walk, he was in a wheelchair.

Grace impressed me, her sweet voice, she was as delicate as an Asian doll, I can't even tell how old she was, seventy, eighty, maybe?

The last time I saw her was on the day they moved into a nursing home. Grace seemed sad.

I realized I knew nothing about her, or Korea, I did a lot of research and now I am writing a love story about Mae Lee and Sergeant Lee. It's a sweet love story that grew in the middle of atrocity and defied all the odds."

"Was Grace's husband in the Korean War? Did they meet there?"

"I don't know, Suzy. I don't know if he was in the military, I just spent a great amount of time learning about the Korean War, and that was where I got the idea from."

"Mom, you find inspiration everywhere. I want to hear it. Tomorrow if you like, you could read it to me."

"Like old times... my darling daughter. The outline still needs to be completed, maybe next time you come I'll read it to you."

Suzy spoke about her relationship with Blake, he asked her to move in together. She was afraid I wouldn't support her.

"On the contrary, Suzy, I want to see you married and happy, therefore I agree you should know much better the person that you are joining your life to. Things do change when we live under the same roof, sharing responsibilities. I hope Blake will never disappoint or hurt your feelings."

"Like Dad did to you!"

"Well, I was young and naïve, I really didn't know better, he was my first and only love, I was too needy of affection... With time I believed if I had loved him more, maybe it would have worked better."

"Mom, it was not your fault, Dad is just incapable of real love for anyone, he has proven he is emotionally handicapped. Sometimes I feel sorry for him, he had the best wife he could wish for, and he missed the opportunity of being a truly fulfilled and happy husband and father, you deserved to have a happy marriage and a real companion."

"Suzy, I am fully happy with you and Nicky, you are both heaven's gifts. My life is fulfilled!"

'And my soul shall be joyful in the Lord.' Psalm 35:9

The next morning I was sitting under the sycamore tree, with a pad in my hand, taking some notes, when Rebekah came with Goldie.

"Hi, Ellen, I see you are writing!"

"Yes, this will be my second book, my daughter is anxious to hear this story."

"I saw your daughter leaving yesterday. She is lovely. Tell me more about your family, Ellen."

"Suzy is currently working in Silver Spring, Maryland with a publishing company. She went to college close to home. I see her often. We are bonded!"

"Nicholas, my son, went to Virginia Tech, and after that he found a job with a government contractor in Washington, DC, I am happy he stayed close by."

"What about your husband, Ellen? You hardly talk about him... I only saw him a few times coming out in the morning, he didn't seem too friendly. Sorry to say that. He didn't even look at me."

"I know, that's his way, Craig doesn't talk much. He is only focused on his job, and he is in a hurry when he leaves for work, he has a long commute."

"Where does he work?"

"Craig is at the international airport, far west from here. He is a Tower Control Supervisor. He loves his job."

"Did you always live in Virginia?"

"No, we moved from Maryland when Craig had this work opportunity."

"What about your family, your parents? Any siblings?"

"My father died when I was ten, then I lost my only brother when he was in high school.

By the way, my father, a wise and wonderful man, was half African American. My mother was white."

"You don't say! You don't look biracial at all! What about your mother? Is she alive?"

"I don't know what happened to her, she left when I was eighteen... I had looked for her, didn't find her, I never had any closure."

"How sad. That's all you have to tell about her?"

"Yes, unfortunately, not much to tell...

I lived a small life in the same place, just working, being a mother, doing nothing to be noted, having very little social interaction. Now I distract myself writing about places I have never seen, people I have never met..."

"I disagree, Ellen, you don't live a small life, you create art, you think and write, you are living to the full extent!"

In a matter of weeks I was ready with the script of my new story. Suzy came to stay with me, and on Sunday morning after breakfast I was ready to read it to her.

"There we go, Suzy, I named it 'Sounds of my Homeland.'

In August 1950, Alistair Lee, a soldier from Kansas, was deployed with his battalion to South Korea. They knew of an invasion from communist North Korea into the Republic of South Korea, and the United States was joining forces with the South Korean army to fight the invaders.

Lee and the other young soldiers could not have imagined what they were about to be part of, they had very little understanding of what was happening in that country.

The US Air Force destroyed bridges, stopping most daytime roads and rail traffic. They were forced to hide during the day and only move at night. Bombardment destroyed the city of Incheon. Since the first days of the war, numerous atrocities and massacres of civilians were committed by both North and South Korea. It was chaotic.

Visible destruction, remains of railroad engines and cars along the tracks, villages decimated and deserted... It was hard to believe they were places where people used to live, raised their families.

The weather was inclement, very defined seasons, subject to monsoons and very cold winters, making survival difficult.

The US Army soldiers started losing hope of ever coming out alive...

Thousands of them were killed or missing in action, their bodies were never recovered.

The refugees, trying to flee from the northern part of South Korea, were killed by the thousands by air attacks, including tragically, by friendly fire.

Thousands of South Koreans fled to the south, an estimated five million became refugees. As the cavalry withdrew southward from No-Gun-Ri to the eyes of the soldiers it became a common sight to see bodies lying on the side of the roads. Civilian deaths were countless in that brutal conflict.

During one assignment Sergeant Alistair Lee and his battalion were driving down a crowded road, watching the silent migrants walking and falling down, trying to get to a city away from the conflict. Lee saw among a few lifeless bodies a girl with a baby harnessed to her back on her knees on the gravel, trying to get up to continue walking. She was alone, she looked gaunt.

Sergeant Lee left the Jeep on an impulse and tried to lift her up, he gave her water from his canteen, and touched the young child hanging on her back, it was a little boy, he was dead.

Lee tried to tell her she had to let the baby go. She couldn't understand, she didn't speak a word of English.

One of the soldiers approached them, he could speak a few Korean words. The girl looked at him and refused to give the baby up. That was her little brother, the only one left from her family, she didn't know where she was going.

Sergeant Lee removed the baby boy from her back and showed him to her, she couldn't carry him around any longer.

The girl was exhausted and devastated, she embraced the child, she couldn't cry or speak. She just held him.

Sergeant Lee went back to the Jeep and brought a blanket, wrapped the child in it and placed him in a ditch. The girl kneeled beside him and silently prayed, then she laid on the ground in a fetal position.

The other soldier told him she was ready to die to keep her little brother company. Sergeant Lee was touched, he had been hardened by all the atrocities he had seen so far, but in that moment he felt compelled in saving one life, that girl's life in the midst of so much death and destruction.

He held her in his arms and brought her to the Jeep, he put her in the floor behind his seat and covered her up. The soldier called his attention: "Are you out of your mind? We can't take her."

Lee continued driving through the difficult road along the river Han, and hours later arrived at a station of command, he managed to keep her hiding in the Jeep. He brought her food, and let her sleep there.

The next day he started asking around if anyone knew of a camp for refugees in that area. There were none. He hoped to get to a village and let her be with the residents, he tried place after place just to find more destruction. He continued to his destination, carrying her along.

Days later the girl hadn't said a word. The soldier told him:

"You are going to be in trouble. Imagine what would happen if every one of us would get a refugee. That's not our role here."

Lee didn't listen. He tried to communicate with the girl, he estimated that she was about ten years old. He pointed to himself and repeated his name, until she understood and pointed to herself and said, "Mae-Jin."

He wondered if she had any family left, what would be of her? Maybe she would be lost in a crowd of orphan girls walking the streets of Seoul, looking for food and a roof to spend the night, under any conditions...

He felt great compassion for that child. There were thousands of Maes around, he could not help all of them but maybe he could help just that one, he was determined to find shelter for her to continue living and growing.

Close to their camp, in a small village, they found a convent with some missionaries that were there to help and teach the people. He thought that was a good place to let Mae stay. She held on to his hand and begged him to go with him. The missionary acted as their interpreter.

He promised he would come to visit her every time he could.

Mae fell on her knees and profusely thanked him, for the care and for the food he had given her.

Lee was touched and asked the missionary how old that girl was. To his surprise she told him, sixteen!

"Sixteen? Impossible, she doesn't look more than ten!"

"Undernourished!"

He went on with his duties, fighting many other battles and more and more misery. About three months later, during a few days of leave, he came back to see Mae. She was thriving, looked stronger, and was spending all of her time with the younger children.

To his amazement Mae had learned a few words in English. He motivated her to continue learning, and told her that after the war was over she could go to Seoul and find a good job if she knew one more language.

This time Alistair Lee felt a profound affection for that fragile, delicate girl, not an attraction as a woman, but the most profound feeling of wanting to protect her like a big brother!

Two months later he returned. Mae had written a note to him with the words she had learned. 'My savior, I will keep you in my heart until the end of my time.'

The missionary told him they would probably be moving further south to another mission in a safer area.

Lee promised Mae he would find her. He was determined to follow her progress and help her any way he could.

Alistair Lee went back to the battlefield. He had been in that horrific war for over a year, he was exhausted of seeing so much destruction and horror.

He returned to see Mae in the new location where the missionaries taught the children to build beautiful chimes, made out of bamboo with metal pendants of shrapnel. Mae gave him one and told him when he would go away to his home he would remember the beautiful sounds of her homeland...

Lee didn't know when he was returning to America or when the war was going to be over, but he realized Mae was someone he wanted to keep in his life for good. He gave her his parents' address in Kansas, USA, in case she wouldn't see him anymore. He told her he did not live in Kansas but his parents always knew where he was.

They said goodbye.

"Mae, I'll see you again someday." She smiled and said, "I thank you, I love you."

Sergeant Lee was seriously injured in 1952 and moved to Seoul, from there he was returned to the USA for treatment. He suffered a series of operations.

When the war was over he was still in a VA hospital in a phase of recovery and therapy. Due to his injuries he could not return to active duty and took an administrative job in the Army base in Kansas to be close to his family. He would often think of the Korean girl. Would she remember him? Did she survive the war?

'Someday I'll go back to Korea, and I'll look for Mae!'

In 1955, Mae sent him a letter, addressed to his parents. She was in Seoul with the missionaries who were requesting funds from the government to look over thousands of orphans of war.

In the letter she said they would stay in Seoul for a while until setting base elsewhere. She never forgot him, she prayed for his happiness every day.

Lee never received that letter. His father, thinking of the trauma his son had gone through and what he suffered in Korea, and about to be married to his high school sweetheart, wanted to protect him, so he put the letter in the bottom of a drawer and totally forgot about it.

Sergeant Lee got married and was transferred to Washington, DC Foreign Affairs. The first two years were difficult, his wife didn't like the city, she missed Kansas. In consequence of his injuries and the extensive operations Lee couldn't have children. She was frustrated. They divorced.

Finally in 1958, Mae's belated letter was placed in Lee's hands. His father had passed away and his younger brother found it among their father's papers and handed it to him.

He was shocked! Mae had contacted him, if he had known then he probably would have gone back to Korea to see her! He never forgot her, he had a special attachment to her, like with many of his friends that went through that devastating experience together. Only one who lived through that could understand...

He longed to see her delicate small face, to hear her soft voice. 'How was she now? Married? With children?'

He felt a rush of hope, a connection that had been broken but still was alive in him. He immediately wrote to her, explaining why it took so long, and he was anxious to know more about how she was.

He looked through his Army trunk and found the chime she had given him, he brought it outside in the wind, and remembered her words, 'the sound of my homeland...'

He waited and waited, four weeks later the letter was returned. Wrong address. He wondered, Mae probably didn't stay long in Seoul. Where was she? He decided he had to go and find her. He had to tell her he never forgot her!

Lee took three weeks of vacation and flew to Seoul. Immediately on his arrival he went to the address in the letter. It was a government building, he was informed that years before they housed some officials and a commission to grant them asylum for refugees of war. And, since then, they were assigned new posts elsewhere in the country.

He insisted on records, names of the missionaries that had been there and where they were assigned to, to no avail.

One government employee told him of villages where they had facilities, one was Pyeongtaek. He could write them to see if Mae-Jin was there.

Write? No! He decided to travel to Pyeongtaek by train, it was close enough, about one hour. He was excited! 'She'll be there!'

As he arrived at the village he immediately went to the address they gave him. They were not there, that facility housed an office for the province's government.

They indicated that further in Daejeon, Central South Korea there was an orphanage that housed minors.

That was a longer and more arduous trip, the destruction of war was still visible, reconstruction was on the way, there were many detours. Lee couldn't get there that day.

He was only thirty five, but not the same man, he had difficulty walking, he rested and continued the next day. He rented a Jeep, arrived in Daejeon and found the building.

He anxiously waited in a reception area until a young teacher came in and greeted him. He asked if she knew Mae-Jin.

The teacher smiled, looked into his eyes:

"Sergeant Lee, I am Mae!"

He couldn't believe it. That beautiful young woman was Mae! He was emotional.

"Mae! I came to see you. You are so beautiful!"

They hugged, he didn't want to let her go. She was shy.

"I knew you were coming, Sergeant Lee, I was waiting for you all these years."

"I promised you I would come, Mae, I am sorry it took so long. I didn't receive your letter until recently…"

He proceeded explaining how it happened.

She heard him patiently, and calmly responded.

"I always knew you were coming for me. You promised."

"You speak English so fluently, Mae!"

"I never stopped learning, and now I am a teacher."

"Mae, I am going to look for a place to stay in town, while I am here we will talk every day, there is much to be said. I want to learn about how your life has been. How old are you now?"

"I am twenty-four."

"Are you alone, did you ever find any of your family? Are you married?"

"I am not married and I am not alone, you found me now."

"Oh, Mae, life was cruel, to you, to me, to so many… But we are survivors, I never forgot you, the little girl, so frail but so strong."

"Sergeant Lee, would you like to stay here with us? There are many rooms available, as the children grow to be adults they leave for jobs and move out. Would you stay?"

"If it is not an inconvenience I would."

"I'll show you a private room."

As they walked through a hallway, she asked him:

"Were you hurt in the war?"

"Yes, Mae, I was, that's when I was sent back to the US, I had many operations, treatments, rehabilitation, but I am standing!"

"I am sorry, Sergeant Lee, do you have anyone helping you. I mean, do you have a wife?"

"No, I had a wife, but we divorced, I am alone now."

Day after day in that quiet place, short walks to the garden, a mix of flowers and a vegetable garden, most pleasant conversations… Shortly after his arrival she knew everything that had happened to him and told him everything that happened to her, since the last time he saw her…

The missionaries taught her many skills while she took care of the little ones, she enjoyed learning English and soon started sharing what she knew with the children.

She never knew what happened to her family, no one searched for her. The children in the Mission became her family and she delighted herself seeing them grow.

She spoke of the time after the war when they went to Seoul to plea for installations to gather the orphans they had at that time, over 400 children to take care of.

She said one other teacher wanted to marry her, when she turned twenty-one, but she said no, she told him she was waiting for her 'Sergeant.'

"Mae, do you mean you were waiting for me all this time?"

"Yes, don't you know? You found me, you saved me, my life belongs to you. I love you." She would say all of that with calmness and certainty.

"Mae, do you believe we are meant to be together? Until now I didn't know why I always thought of you, and when I received your letter all I wanted was to find you. We always have been connected, neither time nor distance broke our bond. Yes, I do love you too, Mae. And at this moment I can just say, I don't want anyone at my side but you. But I am not perfect, I don't walk fast anymore, and because of the injuries I would never be a father…"

"You are perfect to me, Sergeant. I'll take care of you."

"Do you know what you are saying, Mae, a young, beautiful girl like you attached to me for the rest of your life?"

"Yes, it is like a dream, all I prayed for."

"Wouldn't you feel sad in leaving the children here?"

"The children are growing, and they are leaving. Sooner or later they will all leave for their lives… But I'll never leave them, we are all connected, we are a family!"

"Mae, here these days at your side I feel like life is starting again, I feel renewed, filled with hope. Mae, are you ready to come with me to America?"

"Yes, Sergeant, are you going to marry me?"

"Yes, Mae, let's get married now."

He expedited their wedding at the American Embassy in Seoul, and brought her home.

They lived a beautiful, happy life, completing each other.

Mae loved children, she worked in a pre-school with small children until his retirement, then dedicated herself entirely to him. They moved to a quiet neighborhood and had the most peaceful life.

She stayed in contact with her 'Korean family.' They went back to South Korea countless times over the decades.

They followed the reconstruction of her country up close and saw South Korea becoming the beautiful nation that it is now. Every time they reunited with their 'large family' that only kept growing. Together, they sponsor many of them to come to America.

Mae had entire albums of photos of 'her children' and 'grandchildren,' and she had many stories to tell about them.

With her husband Sergeant Lee, they formed an enormous family born out of the ashes of destruction into unity and prosperity! Their love was extended out of their hearts to many others."

Suzy was surprised.

"Well, well, well, you little writer, you did it again!

You caught my attention, Mom. How did you come up with that idea? It's so unlike you talking about a war… But so thrilling, and touching!"

"The story took a life of its own, I just let my imagination fly high and I didn't feel bored anymore, it was fun to write it!

It will continue… It's a work in progress!"

"Mom, I can only tell you, you don't cease to amaze me. Continue writing, and when you are ready I'll edit it and I'll submit it for printing. You have something really marketable on your hands, your second book!"

"Do you think so, Suzy? I am really happy, my mind is absorbed with this, it definitely helps in my recovery, I feel optimistic!"

When I am alone at home, which is most of my time, I research and look for inspirational readings, there is so much out there. We can find anything on the internet!

The other day I found a hymn with a magnificent choir singing it. It is about the acceptance, resilience of a family in the face of the most cruel losses and adversity.

This hymn, *'It Is Well With My Soul,'* became my daily prayer. In accepting what comes our way, and continuing to hope and fight, we can overcome anything!

I realized that what seemed to be one of the hardest times in my life, the children away from home, a loveless marriage, the layoff culminating with the disease, was actually a blessing in disguise.

Finally I had to put myself first, rebuilding my health. Going through these circumstances I grew in resilience and faith, and I redirected my life. I have nothing to lament or long for, I feel stronger every day, creativity started pouring out of me, I am moving forward!

> *'When peace, like a river, attendeth my way,*
> *When sorrows like sea billows roll;*
> *Whatever my lot, Thou hast taught me to say,*
> *It is well, it is well with my soul.'*

FIVE

My friendship with Rebekah kept getting stronger. She told me that she hasn't had a friend like me in a long time, maybe her entire life, someone that she could talk to about anything, knowing she was being understood.

I felt the same way. There was much empathy between us.

I opened up to her and did tell her I was sad, my husband was not a bad person, but he was insensitive to my feelings and emotionally detached, not only from me but our children, and as a matter of fact, from everyone. He lacked personal connections.

Craig lived in a world of his own, and his only interest was his work at the airport, where he spent most of his time.

His detachment had created a problem in my family, particularly with our son Nicholas. He did not have a supportive father to guide him, they didn't bond. Boys need to have a father to look up to, to share experiences, to learn from. Nicholas always felt that his father did not love him.

I would repeat to my children:

'It is not about you, it is all about him, he has no capacity of expressing love.'

Suzy seemed unaffected by her father's detachment. Sadly, the truth is she never experienced the protective love of a father, either.

"What about you, Ellen? How did you hold up so well, all these years?"

"My faith holds me up."

"Are you religious?"

"I don't think of myself as religious, but spiritual. I pray for strength, I believe, and I hope."

'Now may the God of hope fill you with all joy and peace in believing...'
Romans 15:13

"Ellen, I don't know if I believe in the spirit! I never gave much thought to that."

"I do, Rebekah, and reading the Bible for me is nurturing, it is what I need..."

"You are a very peaceful person with a great heart, Ellen, I love listening to you. In your presence sometimes I feel wicked, beyond redemption."

"Why would you say that, Rebekah? I'm blessed for having you as a friend."

Rarely I saw Colton, Rebekah's husband. Sometimes she would join him for a reception or other events in DC, where he would spend most of his time. But when he was at home she was the happiest.

She told me that Colton was very independent and the way she was keeping him close was to give him space.

He was an impressive man, tall, large build, his hair completely gray, nice features, and charismatic. Several times she told me he was the true love of her life, she was alone for a long time before meeting him ten years ago, and she was looking forward to have a lifetime together into very old age... She was happy with her marriage.

Many months into my recovery there was an improvement in my mobility. The treatment was working, but I still needed to be mindful, mostly on the stairs.

One morning, I felt ready to try, and for the first time I went all the way to the upper floor. Until then I would only stay on the ground floor, and once a day I would go up to the main floor to spend a few hours.

What I saw in the master bedroom made me deeply upset. Craig had transformed that room into his own space, he had his computer desk set up, all of his simulation videos and much more aeronautical paraphernalia I hadn't seen before.

He took away the white, cotton comforter we had on the bed, and the curtains. The room looked stale. A large vase of artificial white flowers I had in one of the corners was gone, picture frames of the children when they were little were also gone...

In the walk-in closet some of my clothes were lumped together in the back. Suzy had brought some of them to the downstairs office that had become my room, temporarily.

In the master bathroom, there was no sign of any of my toiletries, cosmetics, perfumes.

Craig had erased me from that space, I felt he had cancelled me out of his life. Devastation took over me. I went back downstairs and cried for hours...

The next day, Rebekah asked me:

"Yesterday you seemed totally healthy, what happened today?"

I didn't feel like telling her, I would break into tears.

"I'm just stressed out, that's all."

"Ellen, you have to avoid stress at all costs!"

"I know, I want to be in good shape, I have a very important appointment coming up, and I want to hear good news."

"I insist, I'll take you! You do not have to ask your daughter. And, maybe we could stop somewhere nice for a special coffee to celebrate!"

"Thank you, Rebekah, I accept your offer."

With my friend Rebekah I went almost a year after the flare-up, and the doctor confirmed I was in remission, I was thrilled! He explained that remission didn't mean I was cured, and at any time new flare-ups could occur. The doctor recommended that I continue taking medication and moving around, 'Live the most relaxed life possible, stress has consequences, and hopefully you'll never experience that bad episode again.'

That was a great day!

My first calls to share the good news were to Suzy and Nicky!

That evening when Craig came home I was waiting for him in the living room. I had dinner ready.

"Craig, I got some good news today, I am in remission, it can last for the rest of my life or not, we will see, but I am determined to do everything I can to keep this disease away."

He didn't show much surprise, I continued:

"I want to thank you for the care that you provided me with."

"That was the least I could do, Ellen."

"Craig, you provided everything I needed, but no love, affection or company. Are you done with me?"

"No, you are reading it all wrong. I am not affectionate, it's who I am. You are a good wife and an exceptional mother."

"Thank you, Craig, but I am not 'reading it all wrong,' why did you erase me from our room? Did you think I was never going to be able to resume our lives?"

He became angry.

"You know I need time for myself, it always has been this way. I gave up the downstairs space for you, and I needed to have my things together, that's all."

"I know, 'it always has been this way,' and I am tired of it... Once and for all, please explain why. What did I do to you? We loved each other, we had a good start, what happened?"

"You became a mother, and it was all about the children, all your attention was directed to them. I was there just to support the family, nothing else."

"Oh, you finally said it, you were jealous of the children, you were jealous of my attention and love for them. What else did you expect, Craig? Instead of stepping in as their father and sharing the nurturing and care, you resented them! I was alone in that, I worked full time and carried all the responsibilities without your emotional or physical support.

This is nothing but the result of your upbringing, 'the abandoned little boy' that didn't receive the love he needed. As an adult you should have stood up for yourself."

"I do not want to fight about this, Ellen, enough!"

Craig started walking away.

"Please, don't go, Craig, you seem more upset than ever. What else is going on with you? Say it!"

"Nothing to do with you, it's something that happened at work. The executive operational position was opened and replaced with another guy that has much less experience than me."

"I know how dedicated and capable you are, Craig, I'm sorry. Do you know why they chose someone else?"

"Because I am the 'old guy'! They told me that in our profession we don't last long, retirement is around the corner for me."

"Unfortunately, in many cases that is true, but unfair. Why don't you take time off and relax? Maybe there is a better outcome."

"I won't take vacations now."

He walked away, ending the conversation.

I had prepared the guest room for myself, with my most favorite comforter, my children's picture frames, my flowers.

I have my new space and moved back upstairs, alone.

To celebrate my remission I invited Suzy and Nicky to go for a walk at the Mall in DC to visit the Lincoln Memorial.

"I want to walk up all the eighty plus steps again. I can do it with both of you at my side!"

They gladly agreed. I am the luckiest mother, I have the most loving and supportive children, I am counting my blessings.

After visiting the monument the three of us went for lunch. Suzy and Nicky talked about their jobs, friends and boyfriends… I forbade any conversation about my health.

We had a great afternoon, after so long!

Nicholas told us that his job was sending him to the New York office for a long period to replace someone that had gone abroad.

I was not thrilled, I would be seeing him less, but he was happy with the opportunity and the new experience. I supported him.

I reached another milestone, with my Doctor's approval, I started driving, initially only close to home, regaining my independence.

Suzy published my second book, and I told her I was already starting a new story. This one would be intriguing, puzzling, and even sad, but it feels real.

It was inspired by the reclusive lady that lived in the dark and cultivated daisies in the wee hours of the morning, I did not even know her name. I named my story 'Daisy.'

"How did you come up with that idea, Mom? Ordinarily, there's not much to tell about someone who lives such a confined life!"

"On the contrary, Suzy, that is so unusual there might be a reason leading someone to that lifestyle. I saw that neighbor only through a window, we never spoke, but somehow she struck a chord in me, since then I let my imagination take wings.

I really don't have to work on it, just flows!"

"Ok, Mom, I'm curious, let me know when you are ready."

I became absorbed with it, and in a few weeks I had a story lined up, grateful for having all that time available on my hands to do it.

I shared it with my daughter.

"This is nothing like I wrote before, it is not finished yet, but do you want to hear what I have so far?"

"Sure, Mom, like old times, read it to me, please."

"Daisy is about a rich, lonely, shy woman who lacked self confidence and social skills due to a chronic disease that impaired her of living a normal life.

She was born into a wealthy, dysfunctional family. Her parents were cousins. It was one of those families where people married for money, to keep the wealth among them.

80

Before Daisy they had another daughter that died in infancy. When Daisy was born they were consumed with worries about the new baby.

In her second month the *au pair* took her for a stroll in the carriage in their vast garden. Returning to the mansion her mother observed that the baby was covered with rashes and blisters.

They panicked and immediately called their pediatrician. He recommended a well-known dermatologist to treat the severe blemishes. At just eight weeks old Daisy was diagnosed with photosensitivity, commonly known as sun allergy. The child could not be exposed to direct sunlight.

Her mother went to extremes of keeping the baby in a dark room with heavy curtains to avoid any sunlight to come in, but still from time to time her rashes appeared. They found out the ultraviolet light from lamps could also affect her.

After consulting with their doctor he determined the condition was more severe, called XP, xeroderma pigmentosum, a rare disease causing an extremely adverse reaction to sunlight and also other lights with any ultraviolet trace.

The parents had a pathological reaction to the facts, they didn't get a second opinion and didn't follow the doctor's recommendations, didn't provide the baby with treatments to increase resilience and natural immune defenses.

They felt ashamed of having a child with unusual needs, and literally locked her up in a dark room, hiding her from the world.

Daisy never attended school, never had friends her own age to play with. As she grew up, she was only allowed to be in her apartment, three rooms in the mansion, the walls were all painted black, candles or deemed light bulbs were the only illumination she had.

She grew up in a dark, colorless world. She was allowed to go out on her balcony at night, and she fell in love with the moonlight, the only natural light she knew.

The despair and anguish of the little girl was never understood. She craved normalcy, experiences, and to see the world she knew only in pictures.

She had a governess to take care of all her needs, and tutors hand-picked by her father, coming into her dark world, teaching her how it was outside.

Daisy's parents divorced, her mother moved out. Occasionally she would come to see her daughter, but their relationship was superficial. Consequently, she had a deeper bond with her governess Ethel, more than with her own mother.

Daisy was seventeen when she fell in love with Chase, her personal trainer and swimming coach. He would swim with her at night in the mansion's indoor pool.

She was passionate about him, her first love. He would tell her she was the most beautiful girl he ever met, her white as pearl skin was as soft as a baby's face. She believed his words.

He would describe to her what it was like going to the beach under the sun, breaking the waves, surfing.

Their relationship was approved by her father, but it was conditional. Chase only would see her in the mansion, he could never take her outside their gates. At Daisy's request her father allowed them to walk at night in the property's fenced gardens. Chase accepted his conditions for the sake of spending time with Daisy.

As much as she believed her father only wanted her to be happy, she was actually under his entire control. Disguised as a caring father, he was a manipulator."

"Mom, this is horrible! I mean, this is incredible, seems so real, I am feeling Daisy's pain. How did you learn about this skin disease?"

"It was after I saw the shadow of the 'reclusive lady' protected by tainted glass, I started researching.

Suzy, as I'm writing this story I'm ingrained in it, many times I have cried, it feels sad what parents can do to their children, they destroy them.

Daisy suffered so much, mostly because of her parents' fear and control. But, let me continue…

She was educated, she played string instruments, guitar, ukulele, she loved music, and in Chase's arms she happily danced.

The romance between her and Chase was lasting for a decade. Daisy's father was pleased, and often had private conversations with Chase, who was building a business with his financial help.

For Daisy, Chase meant everything, but she wanted to be part of his world, she wanted to meet other people. She had an enormous longing for living!

There came a day when she had the courage to tell her father she wanted to live with Chase. He firmly declined, telling his daughter he had made arrangements with Chase to maintain their relationship the way it was, and also she would only have access to her trust fund if living in their mansion.

She asked Chase to move in with her, he didn't have to be in the darkness, he could occupy any room in the house, and have parties and friends over, anything he wanted, just to be close to her.

That is when the deception was exposed.

Chase went away telling her he could never, ever live in sickness and darkness. The only reason he maintained their relationship for so long was because of the agreement he had with her father... She was crushed.

Daisy's father finally told her he had financed her affair, and had agreed that outside those walls Chase would lead a normal life, as he did. Chase had been married for four years and had a child.

He never had any intention to marry her, never!

Daisy's dark world of deception and betrayal became even darker and collapsed. The only person understanding and comforting her was her governess Ethel, who had spent many years at her side, and was ready to retire and move back to her hometown. But, Ethel postponed her plan to help her.

Daisy became deeply depressed. In desperation on one sunny day she opened the doors and went outside. She wanted the sun to destroy every fiber of her, she wanted to disappear from the earth. The strong light blinded her, defenseless she fell to the ground.

Ethel found Daisy unconscious, covered by rashes and blisters. She called for help. An ambulance came and took her to a hospital, where she was evaluated by a specialist.

Dr. Aberdeen determined that her immune system had shut down, due to the lack of proper treatment and exposure.

Daisy refused to return home, against her father's will she remained in the hospital for months.

As she became physically stronger, with the support of her doctor and Ethel they found her a lawyer to fight in court against her father. She demanded access to her trust fund to live anywhere she wanted. She would never return to the mansion.

During the process her father became very ill and conceded.

She asked Ethel for help. She wanted to live in a house, surrounded by other houses, with people around, children playing outside, she wanted to live among 'normal people' for the rest of her days.

Ethel found a townhouse in a middle class neighborhood, with a small garden where she could cultivate some flowers. There were no fences or gates in that neighborhood, everyone could come and go freely.

Daisy knew that her condition would never improve, she would not be out in the daylight. Ethel moved in with her for one year, before retiring. During that year she taught Daisy the survival skills she needed. Daisy learned how to cook, clean, how to use appliances. She made radical changes in her life.

Dr. Aberdeen also became a good friend and supporter, and with her lawyer, a financial advisor and Ethel they formed a team to assist Daisy. She had the house remodeled to her taste and convenience, she wanted the walls to be white, all the glass windows were shielded by a UV protection tinted film that let light in, keeping the harmful rays outside. It was dark enough from the outside that no one could see inside the house, but she could see the people out there. She would come out late at night, especially under the moon, she felt free and experienced life!

In that house Daisy lived until her last days, she left a legacy of writings about the beauty of the world, the values of freedom that most of us take for granted. It was amazing to see how someone who grew up under total control and limitations broke those chains and lived!"

"Oh, Mom, That's so sad… But it is poetic! The freedom to live!"

"I become emotional when I'm writing it, Suzy. But this is not all sad, the stories that Daisy left are filled with inspiration, it does end on a good note."

During those months Rebekah and I always found time to talk or meet at the garden, me with my notepad, writing, and Rebekah with her sketchpad, drawing, accompanied by Goldie, now a full grown, beautiful dog laying by her side. She had an idea.

"I have been thinking, Ellen, I want to display my paintings right here in my house, and I thought of spreading flyers all over the place, at the city hall, supermarket, place an add in the local paper. What do you think? Would you like to participate? You could sell your books as I sell my paintings!"

"What a good idea, Rebekah? I never thought of that. We could invite our neighbors and the community across the road. It would be fantastic!"

And it was, working side by side, helping one another, we organized a very successful event that was reported in our local newspaper. It was so successful that we decided we would do it again next year!

Right after our event Rebekah took a trip to Atlanta to visit Patrick and her grandchildren. They never came around...

Once she told me that her son was handsome and smart just like his father, the love of her life! But Patrick never met him...

"He died."

"So you were a widow before your son was born?"

"I was a widow before becoming a widow... This is my third marriage."

"Rebekah! Two times a widow! I'm shocked, we have been talking for years, you never told me."

"I have stories and secrets to tell..."

I told my friend, "Something is worrying me, Craig is depressed, he is being forced to retire, he is resisting, I can't imagine how his life is going to be afterwards, his job has been his only interest, I am concerned about him."

"Maybe that will turn things around for both of you, you'll have more time together..."

"I don't think so, Craig is done with me, Rebekah, there is no love there. I'm scared of what is happening to him, he has no friends, no other interests or hobbies. Maybe he could become an instructor in one of those flight schools. We'll see."

"Would you move away if he finds something to do elsewhere?"

"No, Rebekah, I am not planning to. I do not know what the future reserves, but I feel that my time with Craig is over.

Throughout my entire adult life he was the only man I loved, and in the end I am alone. He is physically here, that's all there is…. His heart is not and never has been."

"I'm sorry, Ellen, that's not fair. What happened to both of you?"

"It sounds ridiculous, but Craig was resentful of the attention and time that I gave the children when they were little. He was jealous, and instead of being part of their upbringing he went to an extreme and detached from all of us."

Admitting out loud that Craig and I did not have an emotional connection freed me. I didn't have to pretend I had a good marriage.

In an unexpected turn of events, two months later, driving down to the airport, Craig was in a traffic accident and seriously injured.

I was informed by the State Patrol no one else was involved, Craig was probably distracted, speeding. It was devastating!

The second shock I had was when I called his supervisor at the airport and was told that Craig didn't work there anymore, he had retired weeks earlier. And there he was pretending he was going to work every day!

It was not the time to be angry about it, and I stood by him at the hospital in western Virginia.

The first days Craig was mostly induced, couldn't speak at all. He had a head injury.

During that time even if he couldn't hear me I spoke words of compassion. I told him I would help him heal, he was the only man I have ever loved, and I was grateful to him for giving me the most precious gift, a family.

Discussing his status with the doctors they told me he would recover but needed special care after leaving the hospital.

Suzy and Nicky came to see him when he was alert, he bluntly told them to go home, he didn't want any pity! I asked my son and daughter to wait outside.

"Craig, the children only want to help and support you. Are you ready to tell me what is going on? For the past two months you haven't said a word, I hardly saw you, and now I learned you were not working anymore!"

"Ellen, I am not a man of many words. This accident is not going to change my plans, I am moving back to Maryland, to the Eastern Shore. I have it all arranged."

I was shattered, but I kept my emotions under control.

"When were you planning to leave me? Is there another woman?"

"Please, Ellen, no drama. There is no one, I just want to be on my own. You can keep the money we have in savings and the house. My pension and retirement fund are enough for me."

"What about a divorce, Craig? I would rather have this situation defined."

"I do not want a divorce, you shouldn't either, don't be silly. I am trying to be fair, you stood by me and worked hard. I am not doing this to hurt you, Ellen. I just want to be alone."

"You have always been alone, Craig. Unfortunately, you do not have emotional ties with any of us. You do not love even your own children. But, I don't think this is the right time, you need help to recover."

"I am not coming home, I never liked that house, too many stairs, and you have your health issues to take care of. The doctor suggested I'd be transferred to a recovery clinic, I'll go straight to Easton.

I have started packing my aeronautical materials. Please, pack everything I have in my room, closet and bathroom, including my desk, chair and recliner. I'll arrange the transportation."

"Do you want the bedroom furniture or anything else from other rooms?"

"No, nothing else."

"OK, you are well taken care of here, I am going home with Suzy and Nicky. If you need anything, call later."

I was numb, like walking in a fog. It sounded like it was a nightmare. That couldn't be real!

Suzy and Nicky were waiting for me outside.

"What's the matter, Mom? You look so pale."

We held on to one another. I told my children their father was leaving us. He had it all arranged prior to the accident, and I didn't suspect anything.

"I never imagined that Craig would depart from our lives so suddenly. Until now, I did hope that he would have been closer to us. I wish he had loved me."

When we arrived at home Nicholas was angry, he immediately went upstairs.

"He wants his things packed, I'll do it! The sooner he takes it all away, the better."

Suzy and I hugged and cried.

"Dad was never caring, he never loved us. But, it is still shocking the way he is doing this. He is so cruel, Mom. It feels like a death."

I went into profound sadness.

'He heals the brokenhearted and binds up their wounds.'
Psalm 147:3

The following week Craig was transferred to a recovery facility in Easton, as he wished.

I got ill, not like the first time, but still I was impaired of leaving the house for a while.

Again, Rebekah immediately offered me her full support.

She was there, day in and day out, taking care of me. She helped me with paperwork. Surprisingly, Craig had his papers in order, I didn't know he had a life insurance policy in my benefit.

Rebekah suggested I transfer the bank accounts in my name only and get a Power of Attorney to be able to sell the house when I want to.

It was overwhelming, and I welcomed my friend's help.

"Ellen, there are things you need to learn. Husbands sometimes are worth more dead than alive!"

"Rebekah! What are you saying?"

"Sorry, it was just a silly comment to cheer you up."

Craig told me I did not have to come to see him at the recovery center. I couldn't drive that far anyway. When he was ready to be released he sent a van with two men to collect his belongings. I had the address where he was moving to and told him:

"I won't intrude in your life, Craig. If you want to talk or need anything, please call."

Rebekah tried to motivate me, taking me out.

"You need a change of scenery, Ellen. When the weather gets better I want to take you to the Arboretum, have you been there?"

"No, I haven't, Rebekah."

"You will love it, especially that you are a Lincoln admirer, you'll see the columns displayed there."

"I heard about the old 'National Capitol Columns,' is that it?"

"Yes, they were part of the Capitol from 1828 to 1958, and towered over Abraham Lincoln's inauguration. See, I also know a little history. We will see it in the spring."

"Thank you, Rebekah, my good friend!"

After the shock of the sudden departure, I accepted the reality that Craig was not there anymore and there was nothing I could do about it, as a matter of fact I didn't want to do anything, I was fine without him.

Suzy and Nicky came often to see me, for a while they were angry and sad for the void their father left in their lives. But, soon they stopped talking about what he did.

My son announced he'd be moving back to DC permanently. He still would go to New York City occasionally.

"I want to be close to you, Mom! Enough of being away."

I was delighted.

Spring arrived, and as promised, Rebekah accompanied me to the Arboretum. 'Life goes on...'

It was a splendid day of blue skies, blooming flowers. I was feeling well, walking steadfast, enjoying the day.

I was fascinated by the display of the twenty-two columns, artistically placed in an open meadow.

"Lincoln stood under these columns twice, on his first inauguration in 1861, and second in 1865, to a war-torn nation, he said:

'With malice toward none, with charity for all, with firmness in the right as God gives us to see the right, let us strive on to finish the work we are in, to bind up the nation's wounds, to care for him who shall have borne the battle and for his widow and his orphan, to do all which may achieve and cherish a just and lasting peace among ourselves and with all nations.'

Just thinking that only forty-two days after this he was gone, assassinated... Oh, the cruelty of life!"

"It impresses me that you know so much about President Lincoln, Ellen."

"Since early childhood... It is my father's legacy to me, a memory to last forever."

Rebekah took some pictures. She was going to make a painting.

What a beautiful day!

As time went on, we accepted the reality that Craig's time with us was over.

Suzy came to see me and stayed overnight for the weekend. She asked me:

"Did Father ever call? Not that I miss him!"

"No, I haven't heard from him. He knows he can call any of us if he wants."

After that conversation I did call Craig to ask how he was doing. It had been a long time...

He was short in his answer, saying he was alright and was working part time at the local airport. He didn't ask anything about us.

Next time I saw Rebekah I told her:

"My daughter and son are alright, how could they miss what they didn't have? But I still have a hole in my heart, mostly for the sudden way he left. Sometimes I feel like a grieving widow."

"I know what you mean, Ellen. I was a widow, but I felt relieved they were gone, my previous marriages were wrong, wrong reasons and wrong men. I'll tell you one of these days, it's a long story..."

"Real life stories fascinate me, Rebekah."

For months I had neglected my writing, and Suzy reminded me that she was waiting for my Daisy novel, to edit it.

"I'm sorry Suzy, for all these months I was consumed by Dad's departure, dealing with my feelings and everything else, but I am moving forward, I will finish it soon, Daisy's story is waiting to be told..."

"You take it very personally, don't you, Mom?"

"I do, for me Daisy was a real person. I owe it to her to make her life and the message she left behind known."

My son had a boyfriend Damian, they met in New York. He wanted to introduce him to me.

"Just like I told Suzy when she met Blake, I'd like to meet him when you decide it is a serious relationship."

I couldn't turn my son down, but deep in my heart I wished I never had to meet his 'boyfriend.' I was not used to the idea...

Suzy and Blake are going along slowly. After years of living together, they have talked about getting married. I was excited by the prospect of a wedding.

She had great expectations for her birthday, which we celebrated with joy! But it was not all happy. She was a little disappointed she didn't get a ring or a proposal, as she expected. And, I didn't have a good feeling when I saw Blake, he seemed a little aloof.

The end of this sad year was approaching quickly.

I went upstairs and looked at the master bedroom. I hadn't been there in a while, the empty room was a reminder that Craig was gone for good, it was final! Unexpectedly, a strong sense of grief took over me. Grieving is a long process, those feelings come and go.

Craig never called me. I wanted him to know that although he had made his choice, I still had hoped that he would reconnect with the children.

I broke the silence and called him to wish him 'Happy Holidays,' and invited him to come to join 'his family' for dinner.

He said he was well and he couldn't come, he had work to do…

I decided right there I would not move back into that room, and this was the right time to put my mind to a new project. I was going to redecorate it, transforming it into a comfortable guest room for Suzy or Nicky to stay when they would come home.

Before going to Atlanta to join her son and family, Rebekah told me she would never stop going back to see him, although Patrick maintained a cold relationship with her.
"I love my son, I'll keep trying, someday he will warm up to me! You'll understand when I tell you about his father…"

She gave me the most special present, a painting of the Lincoln columns at the Arboretum.

Rebekah had given me the first one for my birthday, of my most favorite sycamore tree.
I appreciated one more meaningful gesture of friendship, and treasured the beautiful paintings.

'And the sweetness of a man's friend gives delight by hearty counsel.'
Proverbs 27:9

SIX

After Rebekah returned from Atlanta, she came by and brought some sweet rolls.

"Freshly baked, Ellen, let's have them with coffee and talk."

"How was your trip? Did you have a good time?"

"It was short, but just enough to see how my grandchildren are growing beautifully. My granddaughter is looking more and more like me. But being around my son brought up many memories of when he was a little boy, many of them are sad."

"Is it about his father?"

"It is about everything. The other day I said I wanted to tell you about my previous marriages. Do you have time now, Ellen?"

"Of course, Rebekah, I always have time for you. I am all ears."

"I have mentioned before when I was a teenager I was determined to go to nursing school, my father discouraged me, saying we had no means, then suddenly he changed his mind and came up with a solution.

One of his friends, who he had met many years before working together, had established himself in Charleston as a house painter, and on a visit to Santee he had told my father that he had an eye on me to be his wife.

Tobias Galens promised my father he would provide for me, and I could attend school if I married him. He was twenty years my senior. He was single but had lived with someone for many years, she had disappeared and there were rumors that he had something to do with it, but my father, being the good man that he was, dismissed those rumors.

I knew that in Charleston there was an accelerated nursing program, and I was thrilled with the possibility. Arranged marriages were common in my family, I did not want to get married to someone I hardly knew, but that was the only way to leave poverty behind and achieve my dream, I agreed... As an ambitious eighteen year old, I didn't have the maturity to foresee the consequences.

I married Tobias and went with him to Charleston, with rare visits back to Santee to see my family.

Tobias was controlling, nevertheless I was committed to our agreement and to my school program, but very soon he became abusive, and as time went on he started assaulting me, demanding demeaning sexual favors, hitting me, telling me he owned me, I was his property, because he was paying for me to be there.

I was inexperienced, but I knew that marriage should not be that way. My only example were my parents, Father never mistreated Mother.

Life with Tobias was torturous, anyway I continued hoping that upon graduating I would escape, working as a nurse. I got pregnant, he didn't want any children and he forced me into an abortion, which was horrific. I was only twenty years old, didn't want to have any children with him, but as a pediatric nurse I loved children, and became very resentful and conflicted."

"Oh, Rebekah, that was traumatic! You were too young to go through something like that."

"I hated him with all I had, but I couldn't leave, I had to finish my course. I graduated and started working at the hospital. At that time Tobias demanded that I give him all my salary to start paying him back.

I couldn't stay with him anymore, I begged him to let me go. He would hit me violently and make death threats, saying that he knew well how to make someone 'disappear' like his old girlfriend... I was terrified.

That nightmare lasted for a couple of years, I worked as much as possible in double shifts to stay away from him while Tobias enjoyed the extra money I would bring home.

In the course of that time I met a young doctor Logan, he was an intern in the hospital, and we fell in love. For the first time in my life I knew what loving a man was and hoped that we could be together, as he promised me.

I was hopeful the solution was right around the corner, I was determined to run away with Logan. But, life worked its way.

One day when I returned home after working ten hours, I found Tobias in the same position I had left him in bed in the early morning. He was cold. He was dead. A massive heart attack!

I was free. But not entirely..."

"Rebekah, what a sad story! Sad and horrifying! Your life was certainly eventful, but what happened to you and Logan? Did you marry him after Tobias was gone?"

"No, it didn't happen how he had promised. Logan ended his internship and returned to his state of Colorado. He went away without knowing I was pregnant with his baby."

"He didn't know about the baby?"

"No, I was in shock he was leaving me, that was not what he had promised. I never heard from him again."

"Oh, Rebekah, how old were you then?"

"I was only twenty-two, brokenhearted, pregnant and alone."

"I can imagine how difficult it might have been. How did you deal with all of that alone, Rebekah?"

"I had to think of the baby I was carrying, I didn't waste any time, moved to another side of town and decided to get a car to transport me to work. I was tired of depending on public buses, especially in the wee hours of the morning.

At a used car lot I met Neil. He was a charming salesman, in a brown suit, his hair plastered with gel. After an hour of conversation, he gave me a good deal on a car and asked me out.

I told him I was recently widowed, pregnant, in no condition or interested in dating anyone.

He insisted he just wanted to be my friend. We had a platonic relationship, which was very comforting to me. I desperately needed a friend! He was kind, gentle mannered, perfectly groomed.

Right after Patrick was born, Neil asked me to marry him. He loved children and wanted to be part of my baby's life, being his father. He told me that he had 'a defect' and would never be a father, but we would support each other throughout, raising my baby together as a family.

He liked me, I liked and trusted him so much that I even told Neil the truth, that my son was another man's child, not my late husband's."

"Rebekah, does Patrick know who his real father is?"

"No, I never told him, I was certain he only would benefit from having a Dad. I married Neil with one condition, that he would officially become my son's father and would never, ever tell him the truth.

That mistake still weighs on my conscience. I thought that being the best of friends, united we would raise 'our son' to be a happy boy! That was my only intention.

We got married, moved into a house, Neil continued selling used cars only part time to take care of Patrick while I was working long hours, which meant more money for us…

Neil was patient and devoted with the baby to an extreme. Pat was the happiest baby. Seeing my son growing up happy was all worth it!

By the time Pat was one year old I was working longer hours, and Neil less and less. He said, 'Those were hard times, he couldn't sell any cars…'

He was spending much more time at home, watching Pat, and started drinking excessively. I did not support his vice, especially that I entrusted my son to his care, I urged him to get sober.

As years went on I was stuck with a man that became financially dependent on me, I was paying all the bills, while he would stay at home with my son, giving him the most time.

Pat had a full-time father. Which little boy wouldn't feel happy with all that attention?

Neil was an alcoholic, I was concerned. It was a terrible example for Pat. As I insisted that he stop drinking, find a job, he became belligerent and purposely undermined my relationship with my son, telling Pat that I was intolerant and too ambitious, I was a 'workaholic' putting my job ahead of anything.

Pat was a little boy, he could not understand that I was not there with him because I needed to work to support our family.

In the meantime Neil would take him to his soccer games, fishing, to the park, everything and everywhere, without me.

As Pat grew up he was getting more and more bonded to 'his father' and less to me… That broke my heart.

Neil became diabetic, requiring insulin treatment, but still he would drink vodka. 'Just to wet my mouth' he defiantly would say. He kept a bottle hidden in the fridge.

I told him over and over he was risking his life mixing alcohol with insulin, it could be deadly. He would ignore me, like I didn't know what I was talking about.

Our fights became uglier, and quite often I asked him for a separation. I couldn't keep up with him and his rudeness, and robbing me of my money, and most of all of my son's affection.

I wanted out of that toxic situation. That's when Neil threatened me, that if I insisted he would tell the truth to Pat, that his mother was a 'whore!' And that I always chose money over spending time with him…

I was devastated. That was not true, I loved my son above anyone or anything, and if I was working so hard it was to support all of us. Neil was a dead weight.

I had known for years that I had married another controlling, abusive man. I didn't know better, I was trapped again.

The constant fights were unsustainable, Patrick took sides, defending his father. I still remember his words:

'You are mean, Mom, he is sick, he can't work, you are very disrespectful to my father.'

I begged Neil for an amicable divorce, even offered him financial support and letting him share custody of Pat.

Throughout those years I had grown professionally, had a specialty, I felt that with hard work I could afford my way out of that situation…

Didn't happen that way, we were still together until my son was fourteen years old.

I allowed Patrick to go on a camping trip for a week.

Just three days after he left I found Neil lying on the kitchen floor, dead. A bottle of vodka, almost empty, was on the counter next to the vial of insulin. He drank himself to death, literally!"

"That's so tragic, Rebekah. It's hard to admit but I can understand why you didn't grieve for any of your husbands…"

"I did not, but I closed myself off to any other relationship. The only person in my life was my son,…"

"How did Patrick react when Neil died?"

"He was devastated finding out his father was in a morgue waiting for burial. He didn't get over the fact he was not there to help. 'Maybe if he were home he could have called for help, he could have saved him.'

I tried to console him: 'Dad was really ill, no one could help him. I am here for you, son, I'll do anything to make you feel better.'

In an attempt to improve my son's daily routine we moved close to his new high school, I changed my work schedule in a way that I had time to attend many of his activities and games.

Sometimes I didn't get any rest at all, going straight from my night shifts at the hospital to the school or soccer field.

My free time was all for my son, I didn't have any social life or friends, despite all my efforts Pat didn't bond with me, he missed his 'Daddy' and talked about Neil very often. For me he had harsh words…

'You were mean to him, Mom.' 'He was just sick and couldn't work, but he was fun to be with.' 'My Dad loved me.' 'He was the best father.' 'Mom, you don't understand!'

That was cruel, it hurt! For me it was punishment, but I listened to him, validating his feelings and at the same time thinking he was just a teenager. He had no perspective of the real facts, and he didn't see how Neil abused me.

I kept hoping that was enough to turn my relationship with my son around. I could not bear to hurt Pat even further, telling him Neil was not his real father, and I let him idolize his memory..."

Rebekah broke into tears. I tried to comfort her.

"I am so sorry, Rebekah, life is cruel sometimes. You were young, too young to foresee the consequences... But, Patrick should know who his real father was, maybe not when he was a young boy, but as an adult, you should not have hidden the truth. Sorry to give my opinion, I am all for the truth!"

"You are right, Ellen. There is more, much more weighing on my heart, I don't have the courage to say it out loud... I wish those memories would be burned."

"I understand, Rebekah, just talk about what makes you feel better, let go of those feelings."

"Yes, Patrick did wonderfully in high school, and getting closer to his graduation he announced he was applying for colleges only out of state, he was moving away from South Carolina.

He was accepted at Georgia Tech, he was going to Atlanta.

I was devastated, I was about to lose my son.

A former co-worker of mine had moved there, she loved the city and told us of great job opportunities.

With not much doubt I decided I was leaving South Carolina and my long-term career to be close to Patrick. When I told him, he didn't like the idea. He said he was not going to live with me, he wanted to be independent, be on campus, and make new friends.

I was disappointed but respected his will, I just wanted to be close and available to him. My son was my only family!

I succeeded finding a job in Atlanta and I liked living there. During his college years Pat would visit me occasionally. I saw him growing into a handsome young man, I was available and close to be part of his life, whatever little time he had for me I welcomed.

But, there was always some distance between us, the bond that he had in his childhood with 'his father' had never been broken, he revered Neil's memory."

"Rebekah, when did you move away from Atlanta?"

"That happened ten years ago when I met Colton. My son was already thirty years old, father of two, he had married right after graduating a girl that had a big family where he integrated really well. They were more of his family than I was. Despite all my efforts, my son and I never bonded as I worked and wished for. Patrick and I had nothing but a cordial relationship.

I was alone and accepted Colton's courtship. I still remember the impression I had the first day we met. What an outstanding man!

I attended a social event during a conference of pharmaceutical companies, he was a former director of one of the larger ones and at that time acting as a lobbyist in Washington! He lived in DC, was divorced, had two adult sons.

Colton was interested in me right away, which flattered me.

We started long distance, he came many times to see me, I traveled to DC to be with him, he introduced me to his friends. All was perfect, and a year later Colton proposed, he wanted us to move to a house in the Chesapeake Bay, by the water. He offered me an exciting new life!

He was and still is a fine, charming man, I was a fifty-three year old lonely woman, and for the first time in my life I was in a true, loving relationship! I gave myself the chance to be happy."

"Rebekah, I am happy for you, after so much disappointment and suffering, you have the marriage you deserve."

"The truth is I often think I don't deserve it, some dark past memories torment me, they haunt me... I wish I could forget them."

"You have to let them go, move forward, Rebekah, the past is gone, you just have the present, live for today!"

"Unfortunately, it was not all roses, Colton's sons immediately opposed me, without even knowing me they called me a gold digger and demanded their father give them the rights to everything he owned before marrying me.

To satisfy their demands Colton agreed in part and gave them the property he had owned with their mother. But he was keeping his apartment in DC, and eventually he would buy us a house at the Bay, after we were married.

He also asked me not to work anymore, he wanted me to be available to him, to accompany him on his trips and conferences. I couldn't give up completely, I had planned to work until retirement and I got a part time position at the Children's Hospital.

We rented a house on the Bay, where we spent many weekends. I loved the area, the nature views reminded me of my place in South Carolina, and I started a hobby, painting. Never in my life I had time for that! I was spending much more time at the house alone.

I was surprised when one day I returned to our DC apartment and found Colton with a young woman. He told me he respected our marriage, but the company of young women kept him young. He was not happy aging.

We had a fall out, he told me it was partially my fault, I was leaving him alone too frequently. That's when I decided to quit my job, gave up the Bay house, and looked for this quiet community, closer to DC.

Here we are enjoying our life, spending much more time together. I have to say that I do overlook Colton's shortcomings for the sake of our marriage, I do love him, in many ways I feel like he is my first and only husband, with whom I'm growing old together.

"But, are you OK with Colton still spending time alone in DC?"

"I don't mind, he is loyal to me. I am not lonely here after I made a new friend, you, Ellen. I really treasure our friendship."

"I do too, Rebekah, you have been very supportive of me, mostly during the difficult times, even right now with your conversation you made me forget my own issues. Thank you for sharing it."

"Are you going to use any part of what I told you in your stories, Ellen?"

"I won't! I don't write about real life, it is all fiction. But you are a rich source of inspiration, Rebekah, that I can say."

We continued being the best of friends. After that conversation I saw Rebekah under another light. I thought she was a very strong woman that had experienced the unthinkable in her younger years, but succeeded, completing her mission of raising her son the best way she could, and in the end, found happiness. She just needed to let go of the dark memories…

That summer, on July Fourth Colton and Rebekah were invited to a celebration in DC. She stayed overnight for fireworks and a concert, and returned the next morning alone, which was not unusual.

Colton stayed, but he would be joining her on the weekend to go to the Chesapeake Bay for a barbecue with some friends.

She invited me to come along. She wanted to introduce me to new people, I thanked her but declined. I was not ready to socialize with people I didn't know.

Two days went by, and Colton didn't come home or return Rebekah's calls. She became concerned and asked one of his old friends to check on him.

He did, and it hit us like lightning. He found Colton dead. Apparently, he had died in his sleep.

Rebekah was in total shock and completely devastated.

I was trying to help my friend and stayed at her side through everything.

"Ellen, I love Colton, and wanted us to grow old together, I wanted him to be by my side until the end of my time. I truly love him, I can't live without him."

"I am so sorry, Rebekah, I have no words. How could this have happened? He was not ill!"

"Colton had been injured years ago, he suffered serious back pain and became dependent on painkillers. He died of a drug overdose. I am sure it was accidental, he didn't mean to, he loved life!"

"That is so tragic, Rebekah!"

"It is punishment! My world is crashing in on me. His sons are blaming me, they asked for an investigation. The Police interviewed me, they started an inquiry."

"Why would they do that?"

"They are greedy, they want everything their father had."

"Nonsense, Rebekah, they will come to terms, they are in shock too, they don't know what they are doing..."

"I am afraid, I had helped Colton in obtaining prescription opioids. I had connections with some doctors. The only thing I am guilty of is getting the meds for him. He demanded, because of his position he didn't want to go to doctors often, and he agonized when he was in pain and would calm down only with his pills.

Colton was knowledgeable and savvy, and was not an addict, I could never ever anticipate he would die of an overdose like thousands of people die every day. Now his sons blame me for everything. They are very influential and well connected men. They are relentlessly pressuring the District Attorney."

I felt sorry for Rebekah, she was having the most painful time dealing with her loss and self-imposed guilt. From then on she was not the same, she locked herself in her house, just crying.

Even Patrick seemed uninterested in helping his mother through that painful time, he did not come to the funeral but called her a few times to know how she was doing. I was the only one trying to lift her up.

"Thank you for coming, Ellen. I feel better when you are here, you can help just listening to me, I have much to tell you. During our years of friendship as I got to know you on many occasions I wanted to open up to you, I need to take things off of my chest. I trust you.

I have a confession to make, it's burning in my heart, now more than ever."

"Confession? You are being dramatic, Rebekah!"

"Ellen, please hear me out, I deserve what is happening to me, I need to tell the whole truth, this is the end for me."

"Why are you saying this? What do you mean?"

"You already know about my first marriage and Logan. And, I told him everything about Tobias, his violent outbursts, his control.

Many times during our relationship Logan saw me covered with bruises. He was revolted and insisted that I leave Tobias. I tried to talk to him to let me go.

Tobias became irate and told me the only way I was going to leave him was dead! He hit me so hard, I had a cut on my face, black and blue bruises all over my body, he kicked me while I was on the floor.

I couldn't work for a few days. I was injured and lied to the staff in the Hospital, telling them I fell down from the metal stairs in my building. Such a big lie!

Logan was desperate, Tobias was going to kill me, he would never let me go. I was trapped, I asked for his help. I felt like I had a death sentence over my head.

He agreed if I would involve the Police, Tobias would retaliate even worse. Logan told me we needed to get rid of Tobias, he suggested that there were ways to do it without a trace. Some medication if applied in wrong doses would suppress breathing, provoking a heart attack.

I knew of those meds, I had no access to them, but Logan had! He said Tobias being a heavy smoker, no one would be surprised if he had a sudden heart attack."

Listening to that narrative it all seemed surreal. My heart was racing. "Rebekah, where are you going with this?"

"Please, Ellen, I need you to listen to me. Logan had a plan, he would get me a vial and the proper needle, I would inject it into Tobias when he was sleeping. He even told me to inject it into a hairy part of his body, like his arm, no marks would be visible, telling me to bring the flask and syringe back to him afterwards.

That would be all, it would be simple, painless, and we would be free to go on with our lives…

I thought for a few days, until the day Tobias assaulted me again, I told Logan I was ready.

He gave me what I needed. I brought it home. Got up at 5:00 am as usual for my shift starting at 6:00 am, got ready, and before leaving went back in the bedroom where Tobias was deeply asleep, his arm was out. I stung him with the needle, he turned slightly but didn't wake up.

I put the empty vial and the syringe in my bag, went to work on the same bus I did every morning, stopped at the hospital, walked to Logan's apartment nearby. He took the vial. All done."

I was dizzy, felt like passing out. "Oh no, Rebekah, you and Logan killed your husband!"

"I did, I was numb, no emotions. When I arrived at home in the afternoon I called the paramedics.

They declared him dead of a massive heart attack. There was no trace, no suspicions. Case closed."

I was breathing shallow.

"Rebekah, I never expected to hear anything like this. I am sick to my stomach, I need to leave now."

"Please, come back, Ellen, I need to tell you more. You are the only person that I trust with this horror that I have been carrying for forty years... I'm so sorry to burden you, forgive me."

Rebekah was crying. I had an impulse to put my hand on her shoulder and tell her I was there for her, but I couldn't do it.

I left like walking in a fog, I didn't know if I could cross the street to go back home, I was shaking. I stayed in my foyer for a while, sitting on the stairs, just breathing. All I could think in that moment was:

'My friend, my dear friend is a murderer!'

I couldn't rest, couldn't sleep. I didn't know what to feel. I was shocked, disgusted, nauseous, like I had been betrayed for all of those years believing she was a caring, nurturing person...

But, she had been! I could not forget that!

She had come into my life like a 'big sister' lifting me up, caring for me, the needy one. Unselfishly, she helped me heal, in the hardest times she was there for me.

As conflicted as I was, I had to understand and be there for her.

I returned to her house the next day.

"Rebekah, I can't even tell you of my feelings about what you did. Please, tell me, why? What do you want me to do with this information?"

"I have had a burning hole in my heart for many years, Ellen. I trust you, I confide in you, you are the most caring and understanding human being. For all I know, nonjudgmental."

"I don't condone you! I can't condemn you either! I am not your judge, Rebekah. I am just human and very disturbed by all of this."

"Please, Ellen, hear me. I beg you!

I thought I could erase that event from my memory.

Logan and I started spending more time together, for a short time I felt hopeful. I was only concentrating on my relationship with him, dreaming of what we had ahead together. We were in love, we were free to embark on our new life like nothing had happened.

I didn't see it coming... I was oblivious and didn't realize that our relationship was changing. Logan told me he was remorseful.

I was anguished too, I should have just run away, but I was convinced it was self defense, Tobias would have killed me.

Logan was ready to return to Colorado and bluntly told me he couldn't live with his guilt, and being around me was a constant reminder... "I will always love you, Rebekah, but we can't be together."

With a broken heart I told him I'd love him forever, at the same time I was resentful towards him for abandoning me, and I didn't tell him I was pregnant with his baby."

"Rebekah! I am trying not to be judgmental, is there anything else you need to say? It's difficult for me to listen to this."

"I do understand how you feel, Ellen, but I need to be totally and absolutely truthful also about what happened with Neil."

"Let's go straight to the point, Rebekah, did you kill your second husband, also?"

"I can say he helped himself! As you know, instead of giving me my freedom Neil threatened me repeatedly that he would tell Pat of his origin, and would not let him go.

I implored, Pat was fourteen, in four years he would be leaving for college, I begged him to let me have more time with my son, away from that toxic environment we were in.

He told me to move out if I couldn't tolerate him anymore, but he would make sure that Patrick would choose to stay with him!

That was probably true, Pat was very attached to the one who bestowed the most attention and time on him.

After that big fight, he became physically aggressive.

When Pat went away on the camping trip, alone at home with Neil I had one more chance to talk to him, trying to make him understand that we couldn't go any further with that farce, pretending we were a family.

He could see Pat as much as he wanted, but Pat and I had to move out. Again Neil yelled, cursed, demeaning me. He was irrational.

I lost hope our situation would ever be resolved in a fair manner.

I reached my limit and decided I wouldn't be robbed of my son's affection any longer.

Neil loved his daily drink of vodka, I brought home two new bottles, put them in the fridge right beside his insulin vials knowing that he wouldn't resist, especially that he was alone all day, he was going to get wasted.

On that first day, he had a seizure.

The next day when I returned from work he was lying on the kitchen floor. The vial of insulin and syringe were still on the counter, and one bottle of vodka, half empty, standing by it. I called the paramedics.

Neil was out of my life. His doctor confirmed he was an alcoholic and had relapsed, even after he started the medication."

I was feeling nauseous again. I stood up and left without saying a word.

At home, I cried.

'She is a murderer, a liar. She had no right to bring this upon me. How could I be so wrong about someone I cared for dearly? Not even in my imagination could I ever compose a story like that. Was everything she told me real?'

I didn't want to see Rebekah again.

Disturbed and immersed in those sick thoughts, I had another restless night.

I stayed in my house quietly the next day reflecting on what I should do. I had conflicting feelings about her of compassion, disgust, revolt, understanding, pity and gratitude.

Deep in my heart I liked Rebekah very much, I missed my friend, but I despised her actions of the past.

I felt like I was on a rollercoaster of emotions, and on landing I was going to get hurt...

I prayed and meditated, I wanted to be fair and just.

I understood the despair and immaturity of a twenty-two year old young woman exposed to so much suffering and abuse, her conflict between love and hate, and her hopeless situation.

I felt guilty, I was abandoning her in her worst time, she had just lost Colton, she was in pain and sorrow, her regrets from the past surfaced, she was desperately reliving her wrongdoings, in admitting and confessing them she was in contrition.

Rebekah was repenting for her sins. I would not judge her, and I would not be her forgiver!

As a true friend I would not turn my back on her, I would help her find redemption and peace. I decided I would come to see her the next morning.

> *'No more shall every man teach his neighbor, and every man his brother, saying, 'Know the Lord,' for they all shall know Me, from the least of them to the greatest of them, says the Lord. For I will forgive their iniquity, and their sin I will remember no more.'*
> *Jeremiah 31:34*

Emotionally and physically depleted I needed to rest.

I walked to my room, looked outside the window, and immediately saw the flashing lights of two Police cars coming down our quiet street, they stopped right in front of Rebekah's house. It was noisy and loud, no one could miss it.

I ran down the stairs and went outside to see what was happening. The couple next door was already out, we walked together to Rebekah's front door.

A Police Officer stopped us.

I asked him, "What is happening, Officer? Is my neighbor alright? Is this a robbery?"

"No ma'am, please stay away, do not trespass."

The neighbors started gathering around, waiting to see what that was all about. I just had one thought, 'I need to help her!'

Two uniformed Officers and a man in a suit went into her house, soon after Rebekah was brought outside in handcuffs.

The other neighbors and I were stunned. The only feeling I had in that moment was compassion. I asked her, out loud:

"Rebekah, how can I help you?"

She looked at me with immense sadness and responded:

"Please, come to see me."

They took her away. I asked the Police Officer:

"Where are they taking her?"

"To our local Police Station."

The Police secured the front door with yellow tape. Officers were inside the house, looking for something. One of them brought Goldie outside.

Phil, our neighbor, took her from the Officer's hand.

"I am used to watching Goldie when Rebekah goes away, I'll take care of her."

"Thank you, Phil, Rebecca will appreciate that."

"Why is she being arrested, Ellen? What did she do?"

"I don't know, Phil."

"Are you going to see her?"

"I will."

"Great! Then you tell me what's going on."

"Sorry, Phil, I won't. By the way I can help take care of Goldie while this is going on..."

I pat Goldie on the head. 'You'll be alright, girl.'

I walked back to my house quickly, avoiding talking to any other neighbors.

The next morning I went to the Police Station. They didn't allow me to see Rebekah. An Officer told me there were no visiting hours, I needed to ask for an authorization to see her, I should return the next day from 12:00 to 3:00 pm. I was disappointed.

"Please, can you tell her I was here? I am Ellen, her friend. I'll come back tomorrow and request a visit."

"That I can do," the Officer responded.

I was allowed to see Rebekah the following day, but we were in a room with a glass partition and needed to use a phone.

"Thank you for coming, Ellen, I thought I would never see you again."

"Here I am, Rebekah. Why were you arrested?"

"I was charged with Colton's death. I did not kill him, Ellen! I loved him, I wanted to be with him forever…"

"Of course, Rebekah. Do you have a lawyer? What about bail?"

"I have a public defender. They will bring me in front a judge for arraignment, they might set a bail, or not. Then I believe I'll be transferred to the County Jail instead.

Ellen, I need to talk to you after they transfer me. Please, come to see me there."

She pointed to the phone a few times, I understood that Rebekah did not want to have our conversation recorded.

"I'll come, Rebekah. I hope everything will be resolved soon. In the meantime Phil and I are taking care of Goldie, don't worry about her."

"Thank you, Ellen, I count on you! My only friend."

At that moment the guard announced, "Visitors, leave immediately."

"I'll see you, soon, Rebekah. I am praying for you."

The next day, a Detective came to my house, he had been talking to other neighbors. First he commented that he knew I had been at the Police Station to talk to Rebekah.

"Yes, we are friends."

"For how long have you been friends?"

"Since she moved to this community, about five years ago."

He asked me point blank:

"Did she offer you any controlled drugs?"

"No, never!"

"We know that you participated in an activity of people coming in and out of her house."

"The activity you are referring to was one or two occasions when she was promoting her paintings and my books. That's all!"

"What has she told you about her husband's death?"

"She did not speak details of how he died until days ago when she told me it was a prescribed medication overdose."

"Tell me exactly what she said."

"She said he was taking painkillers and demanded that she help him get his meds, he would be in agony, he suffered excruciating back pain. But she always advised him to be careful with the dosage. Anyway, he knew of all the risks, Colton was an educated and well informed man."

"Did she ever mention he was suicidal?"

"Not at all, on the contrary, Colton loved life, they planned to grow old together!"

"Thank you for talking to me."

"What are you doing with my information? Am I going to be called to depose?"

"We couldn't use your testimony at trial, it would be hearsay. You didn't witness, you only heard he was addicted to opioids."

"Please note that I did not say he was addicted."

I kept track of Rebekah's whereabouts. Nothing was happening. I went to the Police Station and saw her again.

"How are you holding up? Were you arraigned?"

"Yes, I pleaded not guilty, I have also been accused of making a living for passing drugs… They did not set bail."

"That's ludicrous, Rebekah! A Detective came to my house to ask questions about it. The truth will come out. Did they tell you when are you going to be transferred to the County Jail?"

"Probably next week. After I relocate, I will ask you to call my son. You can get his phone numbers in my phone book, please."

"Rebekah, I have your house key to water your plants when you were away, I'll continue doing it. What do I do with your bills?"

"My lawyer will give you instructions. I am sorry to give you so much work, Ellen. But I really need your help now."

"Rebekah, next time I hope to see you up close for us to speak freely."

My daughter came home.

"Mommy, you have been quiet lately, how are you feeling?"

I didn't tell Suzy what I was experiencing. But I told her I went to see Rebekah in jail and I was very disturbed by that.

"I know she is your friend and you want to support her, but if you feel that bad maybe you shouldn't go back there."

"I have conflicting feelings about it, Suzy. I can't help her get out of this situation, nor does she want me to. I can just listen to her. She is very lonely with no one to talk to. I am the only one visiting her."

"What about her son?"

"He doesn't know she was arrested, she wants me to call him after she is at the County Jail."

"I am sorry you are in the middle of this, Mommy. Go rest now, you will feel better tomorrow."

'Trust in the Lord with all your heart, and lean not on your own understanding; in all your ways acknowledge Him, and He shall direct your paths.'
Proverbs 3:5-6

SEVEN

As soon as Rebekah was transferred to the County Jail, I went to visit her. It was a much better set up, a large room with tables. We could sit across from each other and talk face to face.

There were other inmates and visitors around us. Two guards standing in the room by the entrance and exit doors instructed us to keep our voices down. We were not allowed to get closer.

They brought Rebekah in a jumpsuit and shackles.

I felt like crying when I saw her. She looked washed out, with no makeup, no special clothes, like a poor old woman, far from the elegant woman I knew.

She initiated the conversation.

"Ellen, you are a good-hearted person, my dear friend, I am sorry I have burdened and shocked you, I didn't mean to bring this load on your shoulders, please forgive me."

"Rebekah, it is not my place to forgive you nor judge you, but I do not make any excuses for what happened in your past.

Anyway, I am not turning my back on you, the only role that I may have is to help you find peace, peace for your soul."

"Thank you for helping me, Ellen. Do you believe I am redeemable?"

"Yes, you are, you already started the path of contrition. Sincere repentance will lead you to forgiveness."

"Ellen, you don't know how much I thank you for understanding, I have so much sorrow and regret in my heart, if I could only turn back time, I would have made other choices..."

Tears started streaming down her face.

"Rebekah, the guard is looking at us. Let's change subjects. What exactly do you want me to tell Patrick?"

"Please tell him what happened and where I am. And I did not call him before because the conversations in the Police Station were recorded, I need to see him in person. I am begging him to come to Virginia."

"Your son needs to know all the truth. Are you ready to tell him?"

"To Patrick I will only talk about Neil, including who his real father is, but I will not mention Tobias, for now. That would be between me and Logan."

"It is better not to tell him everything at once, it would be too much. I'll call Patrick tonight."

"Please, tell him I love him, and I need him."

She cried again.

Rebekah was showing humility and sincerity.

"May the Lord bless you, Rebekah. I have to go now."

That evening I called Patrick.

"I am Ellen, your mother's friend. What I am about to tell you happened two weeks ago, your mother was trying not to worry you. Rebekah has been arrested, she is in jail."

"Jail? What's going on?"

"It's a long story, Patrick, your mother is being accused of killing Colton, providing him with controlled drugs. She wants to tell you everything in person."

"That's insane, my mother didn't kill him! I need to speak to her right now, please give me the number, I'll call her."

"No, please, Patrick, all the calls are recorded, she needs to have a heart to heart conversation with you. Your mother loves you, she needs you."

"I'll come to see my mother as soon as I can. Please, tell her."

"I will, Patrick, you may come to my house, I'll take you to the County Jail. And, I have the keys to your mother's house for you to stay there."

In the morning I called the Jail to set an appointment to speak to Rebekah. That happens when we lose our freedom, we need to abide by the rules. I called later at the set time.

"Rebekah, I spoke to Patrick, he is coming as soon as possible. I'll let you know when he confirms."

"Thank you, my friend. It will be wonderful to see my son. Are you coming to visit me this week?"

"Maybe. Today I'll be taking Goldie for a walk, she is going to stay with me for the afternoon, Phil has an appointment."

"I miss Goldie so much. Just thinking that I'll never see her again..."

"I'm sure she misses you too."

I spent a couple of days still dwelling on my own feelings. I felt sorry for her. Was that complicity?

I had a weight on my conscience, which I thought was perfectly human. But, I had to stand strong in my faith, I couldn't waver, that human being who has been the most supportive and caring friend I ever had needed me and my compassion now.

Throughout my internal debate about the situation, I put myself in her shoes. 'What would I have done?' I am not the one that is going to cast a stone.

I went to see her.

"Thank you for coming, Ellen, I have been preparing myself that you wouldn't come to see me again."

"Honestly, this has been a hardship, but I am dealing with it, for the sake of the friendship we have shared. I want to help you, Rebekah, I believe that each person who turns to God in sincere repentance will be forgiven and will find peace."

"Do you believe that's possible for me? I don't know what to do, even thinking how I am going to talk to my son. I am scared he might hate me after he knows...

Did Patrick confirm when he is coming?"

"I didn't hear from him yet. When he comes, just tell him the truth, don't be afraid, the truth will set you free."

On my next visit, Rebekah asked me for another favor.

"Ellen, I need you to find Logan. I never tried to locate him, I didn't want to disrupt his life, but now I have to come clean and tell him about Patrick.

I also want him to know if something comes up with the authorities in South Carolina I will never speak of his involvement. I'll take full responsibility. Logan loved me, he was a good man, he wanted to protect me, and I loved him with all my heart."

"That's all very compelling, Rebekah, but don't make excuses for him, in my point of view he is more responsible than you are, he is the one who gave you the idea and the means to do it.

You are acting now like if you were still a twenty-two year old young woman, battered and emotionally frail. You are loaded with guilt and can't see clearly."

"You are so right, Ellen. Why am I exempting him of his responsibility? I have carried this alone for forty years."

"Even if I find him, would he want to hear from you? Does he have a conscience?"

"Oh, I don't know, you are right, Ellen! But I still want to find him to do right for my son."

"Where in Colorado did he go when he left South Carolina? What is his full name?"

"He went to Denver, his hometown! His full name is Logan Patrick Sauk, he was getting a specialization in cardiology. Please find him, you have the skills, you do much research for your writings!"

"Oh, my writings, Rebekah, since you are here I haven't been writing anything, I have been consumed by all of this."

"Forgive me, Ellen, I have the deepest respect for you. I am asking for your help because you are the only one that understands me and can help me. I feel so much remorse, I need forgiveness."

"Pray for forgiveness, Rebekah."

"I do not know how to pray…"

"The Lord will see the sincerity of your heart, ask him in your own words."

'If we confess our sins, He is faithful and just to forgive us our sins and to cleanse us from all unrighteousness.'
1 John 1:9

It was not difficult to find Logan.

Dr. Sauk lived and worked in Denver for many years, currently he lives and owns a Cardiology Clinic in Colorado Springs. He was married, had three children. His older son, also a doctor, is his partner and works alongside him.

To expedite things I decided to call him to make a first contact. I told him I was calling on behalf of Rebekah Galens, as he knew her in the past. Logan refused to speak to me. It was awkward, I insisted:

"It is very important, Dr. Sauk, I'll send you a letter. Please, I ask you to read it."

He hung up, without saying a word.

I wrote a letter telling him where Rebekah was, and she had disclosed to me they were connected in the distant past. She had something of the highest importance to discuss with him. She was anguished and wished they could talk.

I asked him if he had any feelings in the past for her to please respond and give her the opportunity to discuss it. I didn't feel it was my place to mention Patrick.

In the interim I did tell Rebekah I had mailed the letter to Logan. She was anxious, 'Maybe he will never respond.'

Patrick came, and I took him to the County Jail. He spent the entire visiting hour with his mother. She told him the truth about Logan being his biological father, and Neil's death. And, that I was aware of everything, he could discuss it with me, if he wanted to.

When he came out he was devastated, angry, and told me he did not want to talk about it. He was shocked about what he had heard from his mother. That same day he went back to his family in Atlanta.

I had a conversation with Rebekah, she was very sad.

"I told my son that if I am convicted of a crime that I didn't commit I will resign myself and fully accept the punishment for all of my sins. I'll go to jail with a sense of relief. I have carried this guilt for too long, it is like a thorn in my soul that I inflicted on my own."

I offered her a prayer:
'Do not remember the sins of my youth, nor my transgressions; According to Your mercy remember me, for Your goodness' sake, O Lord.'
Psalm 25:7

About two weeks later Dr. Sauk, unexpectedly, called me.

He said he was digesting the information I had reported to him. He had remembered Rebekah through his entire life, but he had moved on. He asked me if Rebekah had told me about what happened in the past.

I said yes, but I was not going to discuss it. He confirmed that Rebekah was in a terrible situation when they met, he could not help her, he had to return home to Colorado.

I did not concur with what he said, and told him I believed everything Rebekah told me, and he should take ownership of his participation to be able to help her heal from the past.

Logan silenced for a few seconds, then said many times he had an impulse to look for her. The 'mistake' of his youth haunted him, he also needed to heal.

He asked me for the County Jail's phone number. I said no, he could not just call on his time, and besides, all the calls were monitored. He asked me if I could be a bridge between them, relating to Rebekah what he conversed and vice versa.

"Sorry, Logan, but I won't be in the middle of this, what Rebekah wants to discuss should be between the two of you!"

He responded he was considering the possibility of coming to Virginia to see her.

I responded, "Please do, she is a woman that had cared deeply for you, she needs closure, she also wants to make amends."

Rebekah was very emotional when she heard it.

"I hope he comes."

During the next two months legal proceedings were taking place to determine a trial date. My conversations with Rebekah continued while waiting to hear from Patrick and Logan.

"Rebekah, you know how this has disturbed me, I feel I am too involved in your affairs. I'm carrying an unbearable conflict of conscience, keeping your secrets."

"I feel so sorry I imposed this on you, Ellen. Are you thinking you should talk to the Police about it?"

"No, that's not what I mean, Rebekah. It's a moral conflict, and it would not help talking to the Police, it would be all hearsay.

So, I keep asking myself, what do I do with these uneasy feelings and thoughts?"

"Write a book, Ellen, tell my story! That way you'll release it out in the world, and hopefully it will bring you some closure."

"Seriously? You want me to write your story? The whole truth?"

"Yes, I envision you under our sycamore tree, remembering the conversations we had, taking notes. Write, Ellen! You always said the truth doesn't hurt, it's liberating, and that you found comfort in expressing your inner feelings through your characters.

I have only one request, to protect Patrick and also Logan, would you please use fictitious names and places? It is not fair to expose them to public judgment or humiliation. Would you do that for me, and for my son?"

I was surprised by Rebekah's suggestion. I felt more relaxed realizing that I had an outlet to let go of the emotional burden. I decided to write all that was happening in my personal journal.

I continued dealing with my own feelings, wondering sometimes if everything Rebekah had told me was a figment of the imagination of a desperate woman about to lose her freedom!

The reality was that Rebekah confessed to a crime she didn't commit in atonement for the ones she committed. And that was a sincere step towards redemption.

On the weekend my son and daughter came to spend time with me.

"Do you think Rebekah is going to be convicted, Mom?"

"Probably, she admitted that she is the one that illegally provided the drugs to her husband."

"Mom, you have been so anxious lately, I know that what is happening to your friend is affecting you much. We worry about you and your health, is there anything we can do?"

"You both being here is all I need. Despite what's happening my health has been stable. When the trial is over I will relax and I'll return to a normal, quiet life, hopefully."

We spent the rest of our days together talking about ourselves. My son took us out for dinner in a nice cozy place, and he had some news for us.

"I am perfectly happy with my job and my frequent train commute to New York to spend time with Damian, I really like him."

"Would you go to work there, again, Nicholas?"

"I don't think so! I like to be close to you."

"Thank you, son. Maybe your friend will move here."

"Maybe. Do you feel uncomfortable with me talking about him, Mom? I just want you to be part of my life."

"I know, son, I love being part of your life. I feel a little uncomfortable, but I'm getting used to it."

Suzy, my sweet daughter, updated me on my fourth book.

It is a compilation of short stories, mostly funny, of people that would come and go, meeting in a park 'Under the Tree,' the title of the book.

Until I wrote it, I didn't know I had a sense of humor…

"It is ready for publication, Mom, you need to start writing another one again."

"I will, I will! After the storm the light will come… For now I haven't had any inspiration."

I had news for Rebekah.

"Logan called! He will be coming to see you."

"Thank you, Ellen, I am happy! I'll have the chance to ask for his forgiveness for not telling him about Patrick sooner."

"I don't know about asking for forgiveness… Logan has his share of responsibility for what happened, and he is the one that left."

"Yes, he abandoned me in the worst of times…"

Logan arrived.

I had confirmed his appointment to visit Rebekah and met him at the County Jail.

"Ellen, you are the first person with whom I can speak about what happened in the past. Believe me, it cost me a lifetime of remorse, I never forgot it."

"Logan, I am more involved in that story than I want to be. I have just one question, you know how much Rebekah needed you then, did you regret abandoning her?"

"I am sorry I did it. I thought that being with her would open those wounds. I sincerely loved Rebekah.

She had enormous potential as a dedicated and excellent nurse, but her life was being destroyed. I was totally convinced she wouldn't survive in her husband's hands."

"Logan, you were both desperate. But you are the one that manipulated the situation. Intrinsically, Rebekah is a good person, a wonderful friend. I understand what you mean about feeling guilty, you have a conscience, after all."

"Carrying this weight for a lifetime has been punishment enough, I came to apologize to Rebekah."

I waited outside while he visited her.

He came back out later, visibly emotional.

"I feel pain for her. What a tormented life she has lived. It is not fair! I was not there for her and my child. I wish I could make up for it."

"Logan, I hope you put it all in the right perspective, and don't be angry at Rebekah for not telling you about Patrick."

"How could I? I was not there for her.

Rebekah told me to go to her house to see pictures of Patrick and her paintings. She said there is one painting that was meant for me, I should take it along. Can you help me with that?"

"Yes, she had asked me to take you there."

I had no feelings of empathy towards Logan, I wanted to comply only with what Rebekah had asked me.

I drove Logan to the house. He came into the foyer and looked around the tall walls covered with paintings.

"This is an elegant place, how many paintings! Amazing, I never knew she had this talent."

"There were many more, all over the walls on the stairwell. Come up to the living room, I'll show you Patrick's pictures."

Going up, one of the first paintings Logan saw called his attention.

"This is the one she meant! It was our place in Charleston, a little hidden cottage, close to the water, where we did spend some fleeting happy moments... I remember!"

"Rebekah wanted you to have it, you may take it along."

"I will. She meant so much to me. I locked away those feelings and moved on, had a wonderful family, succeeded professionally. She carried the burden and is paying the price, alone."

I showed him a framed picture of Patrick.

He held the frame.

"Patrick! He looks like my second son. I wish I could tell him I am sorry for not being his father, I am truly sorry!"

"He came out pretty good, Patrick is a good man and father. But he is also brokenhearted and confused for what is happening. He needs to heal!"

I called a car service to take him to the airport.

Logan left, asking me to maintain contact with him and let him know of the trial's date.

"I want to be there to offer Rebekah my support. I know she is innocent of these charges."

"She will appreciate it, Logan."

I spoke to Rebekah.

"Thank you for bringing Logan, it was heartwarming to see him, I had no anger towards him, only remembered the love once we shared. I was happy to see what he did with his life."

Learning about Logan's visit to her house and the emotion he displayed when he saw the pictures, Rebekah became more anxious about her son and told me Patrick had the habit of holding grudges.

"I am concerned about Patrick, I think he will never forgive me, I won't see my son again. Ellen, please call him, ask how he is doing, please tell him I miss him, I love him, and I beg for his forgiveness."

"I will, Rebekah, I believe Patrick will come around. About Logan, he was very remorseful for what happened. It was the most horrible mistake he ever made, and he is conscious of it. He took moral responsibility for it. And he asked me to let him know of your trial, he will come to support you."

"He will? That's wonderful! I'll be glad to see him one more time."

"It is taking long, Rebekah, why aren't you hiring a better lawyer, you have the money! With a good advocate you could go out on bail, take care of your house affairs, spend time with your son."

"That money is not to be spent on me. All that I have, the house, my paintings and possessions, it is all for my son and his family. I deserve to be here, but accepting this punishment for something I didn't do is difficult, mostly because I loved Colton and would never, ever harm him."

I called Patrick that same evening and gave him his mother's message.

"I am conflicted and disappointed in her. I can't forgive my mother, she deserves to be in jail."

"She agrees with you, Patrick. I want you to know that Logan was here to see her. He also came to her house and saw pictures of you. He was emotional, he said he is open to meet you."

"I am confused, Ellen. I don't know what is right now."

Rebekah called...

"Come, Ellen, I have news for you! I was offered a plea deal. I don't have to go to trial if I confess to the Judge that I provided the opioids knowing that there was a potential risk to kill Colton. They will lower the charge to manslaughter. I would get a sentence of ten years in jail."

"Ten years, and you are smiling about it?"

"Yes! If they convicted for murder, I could go for life or up to twenty-five years. I don't deserve to walk free, I do accept this sentence! I am sixty-five, who is to say that I will come out of this alive! I will probably die in prison."

"How does that work, Rebekah?"

"My lawyer is talking to the prosecutor, they will discuss it with the judge, and a court hearing will be scheduled soon.

In the presence of the judge I will accept my responsibility and conditions stipulated. They will send me to the State Prison. It is far away… The saddest thing is I won't be seeing you anymore."

"We will still communicate, we'll write letters, and occasionally I'll come to see you. Rebekah, I miss you, your friendship, our talks and walks…"

"Thank you, Ellen. I will call my son, do you think he would be receptive? I hope he would come. I miss him badly."

As soon as I knew of the court date I informed Logan. He confirmed he was coming. I also called Patrick.

"I am not speaking on behalf of your mother. She told me she was going to ask you to come. What I want to say is that your mother loves you very much, you mean the world to her, and having the chance to see you once more will give her the strength to face what's coming. How are you feeling, Patrick?"

"Still conflicted, but the more I think, the more I understand my mother. I have many memories of things that happened during my childhood, when Mother was working and Father, or who I thought he was, would be in the house drinking, spending most of his time with me, having fun, playing, but he was also undermining and demeaning her.

I was a boy, and the way I saw it was that she was too hard on him, but now as a mature husband and father I do understand her frustration, her agony, but I still can't justify what she did."

"She feels the same way, Patrick, and she is taking responsibility for it."

"I am taking that in consideration, and I might come to see her one last time, before they put her away. She is my mother after all, and she sacrificed much for me."

"Above all she loves you, Patrick."

I went to see Rebekah one last time before the hearing.

She had been stoic throughout the process that lasted months, but now she was crying.

"I have instructed my lawyer. I want to leave everything to my son, the house, the money, paintings. He can sell the house. Whatever he wants. But I need to ask you, would you take Goldie out sometimes? You told me Phil wants her permanently. Please keep her once in a while, she is happy with you."

"I have thought of that, yes, I love Goldie, she reminds me of you. She grew up with us, I'll see her often."

I felt compassion for Rebekah, these months in jail transformed the confident woman into a frail and disheveled older lady, her hair was totally gray, and no light in her eyes, only sadness.

She was letting go of everything she had and gave up to fight for her freedom, to repent for whatever she did over forty years ago.

"Ellen, if you like any of my paintings, just take them."

"I have the most special ones of all. The ones you painted especially for me, the sycamore tree and the Lincoln columns... I will treasure them for the rest of my days."

"I have plans, I'll keep painting in prison, and I'll teach my new fellows... I'll be busy and productive."

"Keep working, Rebekah, keep painting, don't allow hope to dwindle. I'll be here, writing, praying for you. I will miss you!"

"My dear friend Ellen, you know me better than anyone in this world, I am very grateful for your friendship. I am sorry I brought this burden into your life, I didn't mean to, but when I confessed to you an enormous load was lifted off my soul, I felt like if you would understand me and forgive me I would feel free!"

"It's not my place to forgive, but I still need to learn why good people sometimes do something horrible! Was it despair? Lack of support? An error of judgment?

Anyway, I brought you a Bible, my favorite book where I always found words of strength and hope. I'm sure you'll find them too, in your moments of loneliness."

"It's beautiful, thank you! Where do I start reading about forgiveness?"

"I couldn't make any marks or highlight it because the guards had to inspect it before delivering to you. But you can look on the last pages, there is a verse finder. Anyway, one of my favorite books has always been the Psalms, by David, they apply to every situation or emotion.

For instance, *Psalm 51:1-2* says:

'Have mercy upon me, O God, according to Your lovingkindness; according to the multitude of Your tender mercies, blot out my transgressions. Wash me thoroughly from my iniquity, and cleanse me from my sin.'

"Oh, thank you, my dearest friend, I'll miss you dearly, and I wish you happiness, Ellen, you are young, and you have much ahead."

"Young, Rebekah?"

"Much younger than me! You are just plain goodness, you deserve the best!"

"One thing I learned, Rebekah, not always we get what we deserve."

Logan arrived the night before the hearing and called me.

"I am in town, I'll be at the court house at 11:00 am."

"Logan, you need to know that Patrick will be there too. He is at his mother's house and he is coming with me tomorrow."

"I don't know how he would feel meeting me. Does he know I'm here?"

"I told him you were coming, but he didn't comment. The good thing is that we are all here to support Rebekah, and it will give her and us some comfort."

In the morning, Patrick and I arrived at the court house together. Logan was in the atrium waiting for us, we approached him.

"Patrick, this is Dr. Logan Sauk."

The men looked at each other and shook hands. It was not a big moment when father and son reunited for the first time. They were both visibly anxious.

Very few people attended the hearing. Colton's sons were sitting behind the prosecutor.

Logan, Patrick and I sat at the defense's side. There was no one else from the neighborhood or any other friend.

Rebekah was brought in shackles, accompanied by two guards.

Her hair was pulled back. She looked at us, her eyes were watery.

She looked at Patrick and whispered, "I love you."

All standing, the judge came in.

The prosecutor presented the plea agreement for manslaughter, recommending incarceration of ten years, and added a special request that her property be assigned to Colton's heirs and her pension be suspended.

We were surprised by that request, it seemed unfair and unrelated to the plea.

The defense spoke briefly, declaring that the defendant agreed with the guilty plea, in terms to minimize the anguish of both families, hers and the deceased. But, he contested the request, there was no merit in taking away what was legally and rightfully hers and her heirs'.

The judge looked at the papers for a short while. He was prepared for his verdict. He asked the defendant to rise and state her plea.

Rebekah spoke with a trembling voice, but she was composed.

"I am guilty of illegally obtaining and delivering opioids to my late husband Colton Wesby. I apologize to his family, and I am prepared to receive my punishment.

Your Honor, I humbly request that after this proceeding I will be allowed to have a minute with my son and my best friend for a last word and a hug, before I go away!"

Her request was unusual and unexpected.

The judge was stone faced, no one knew what he was about to say.

"I warrant the prosecution's plea for manslaughter. I hereby confirm the defendant will be incarcerated for the period of ten years in the State Penitentiary - Correctional Center for Women in central Virginia, deducting the time she has already served at the County Jail.

Regarding the suspension of the pension and the house owned by the defendant I therefore do not grant it. Such property and funds will remain in the defendant's name or whomever she will designate."

He spoke directly to her:

"Mrs. Wesby, I grant you a few minutes with your son and friend, in the cell outside this courtroom.

This session is ended."

Rebekah bowed her head, "Thank you, Your Honor!"

She was humble and seemed pleased with the verdict.

The guards approached and walked with her. Another one addressed Patrick and me:

"Follow me."

Logan told us he would be waiting outside for us, and asked me to tell Rebekah, "She'll be in my heart and my prayers. When she is out, if I am still alive I'll be here for her, I'll be her friend, and I'll support her. I am in debt with Rebekah, I am filled with remorse, I should never have left her..."

An Officer took Patrick and me to an area in the back of the courtroom.

"One at a time," he said, and opened the door to a small cell where Rebekah was waiting.

Patrick told me, "You go first, Ellen."

We embraced, there were many tears.

"My dearest friend Ellen, thank you, thank you for your compassion and support. I truly accept losing my freedom, but it causes pain the fact that I won't be seeing my son and family anymore, and, most of all I am losing your friendship."

"Rebekah, you confessed to a crime you didn't commit in atonement, you will find peace. I am very sad too, I'll miss you, I'll write, and I will come to see you. I will always think of you as my dearest friend."

"Under the sycamore tree..." Rebekah completed.

I gave her Logan's message.

"Please tell him I forgave him."

The Officer knocked at the door.

We hugged for the last time.

"Ellen, you are more than a friend, 'my sister,' I love you. I want you to take good care of yourself and enjoy your life. Don't be sad, and don't worry about me, I'll be alright."

"I love you, 'sister.' May God bless you and keep you."

I exited feeling the pain of losing a loved one. I was crying.

Patrick went in. I waited.

When he came out his eyes were red, he dried his tears.

"You are my mother's best friend, she could not have gone through this without you. Thank you, Ellen!"

"Your Mom is at peace with herself, Patrick, and so am I, but I will miss her dearly!"

The Officers directed us to leave the premises.

We walked together to the atrium, in silence.

Logan was waiting. He couldn't hide his anguish.

"How is Rebekah feeling?"

"Logan, she is making amends with her conscience. She asked me to tell you she forgave you, she's at peace with herself."

He was emotional.

Rebekah's lawyer approached Patrick and told him he had signed papers from his mother regarding the property and everything else that she was leaving for him.

He opened his briefcase and gave Patrick a stack of papers.

"One of these is the deed for the house, it is all yours. That's what your mother wanted."

Patrick was very surprised.

The three of us exited the court house.

Logan told Patrick:

"I am giving you my phone and address, please call me if you want to talk about your mother or about us. I am open to you, Patrick, you are welcomed in my family!"

"Thank you for being here today, Logan. We will talk sometime."

Logan left. He was flying back to Colorado that afternoon.

"Thank you, Ellen. Please keep me informed whenever you visit Rebekah, tell me how she is doing. I would love to hear from you."

Patrick and I went home.

"Come, have lunch with me, Patrick, then if you want to sort some things out in your mother's house I can help you."

"This is so surprising to me, in reality my mother always worked to give me everything. She paid for college, she rented an apartment for me when I started working and did not want to move in with her. I was such a brat!

Lately I have been thinking of my childhood, I can see clearly now how she was abused, demeaned. I imagine how hurt and frustrated she might have been. I was a child, I couldn't understand, I believed what my father said, I mean Neil.

I understand why things ended up the way they did, why she was so exasperated to act that way...

My mother was blinded by despair, she didn't see a way out. She made a terrible choice, but no matter what, she is my Mom and I love her."

"That's all she wanted, the love of her son."

"I told her today that when she is out I'll take care of her. She did everything for me, it will be my turn to care for her in her old age. She'll have me and my family, she won't be alone. I also told her I forgave her!"

"Oh, good son! You are a good man, Patrick."

It had been over nine months from the time of Colton's death until Rebekah's sentencing. Now, it was all over!

Alone at home I faced an overwhelming emotional crisis.

I thought I would never see the light again. It was a time of solitude and reflection.

The day I said goodbye to my imperfect friend I left behind a piece of my heart. I was devastated, mourning for her loss, and still dwelling on ambivalent feelings.

Rebekah was good and evil, the same hands that healed, protected people and produced beautiful art were the same that killed.

How could she have those opposite aspects and still be a caring, loyal friend? It was not coherent or logical.

I wanted to forget about that conflict, or maybe I would start writing a book based on her troubled life, to let all of those feelings out. Rebekah was inspirational, no doubt!

My heart was broken for all the losses I had suffered, but mostly the loss of hope of sharing life with my friend again.

I thought of breaking away from her to terminate my days of mental anguish.

It would be easier to let Rebekah evanesce in the past like she had just passed by, like many others in my life, instead of allowing my emotions to guide me.

But, fairness had always prevailed in my heart, the side of Rebekah that I knew, the true friend, the support, the sharing, the love that she demonstrated, it was the reminder of who she truly was. My friend!

The other, that had taken steps to change wrongdoing, revealing the truth with contrition and remorse, repenting with sincerity and humility, is the one that needs to make amends with her Creator!

I chose love! I followed my heart and vowed to support her in her new way, and made the final decision to never talk about her downfall. I vowed not to share Rebekah's secret with anyone, not even with my own children.

I had done that all my life, looking to what was good, overcoming hardships or painful experiences. Now more than ever, I wanted to have a light and fair heart.

I needed to heal, I retreated into my solitude and cried many tears.

Oh, I wished I had my son and daughter still little in my arms, filling my days with the magic of childhood...

I wanted to ask my daughter and son to move back into our house, to be a family again, but I couldn't. They had their own lives, it was their right to follow their destiny without me.

My husband was not there anymore, but when he was, he did not nurture me, I wished we had had a great marriage, an example to show our children, our grandchildren, a testament of love and communion of souls.

Oh, I had wished in vain for a soul mate, for someone to talk to, to listen to, to understand, to share…

I felt empty and realized the reason I had started writing stories, in my mind I was creating people, lives, voices that filled my days, giving me the impression that I knew them and they were here with me.

My fictional characters filled the voids, the emptiness for the ones that had left. The ones I did not have…

I didn't hope for a fulfilled life anymore.

For now, day after day, I just needed to cry and wash away the heartache.

I know that with faith, the day will come when I'll get up and continue living, I will restore my soul, and hope again…

'Your sun shall no longer go down, nor shall your moon withdraw itself; for the Lord will be your everlasting light, and the days of your mourning shall be ended.'
Isaiah 60:20

EIGHT

My daughter Suzy was also heartbroken.

"Mom, I did not tell you before because you were going through so much. After many years of failed promises, ups and downs, Blake and I broke up. I found out he was lying to me, he was deceitful, insidiously cunning. I can't even describe how much he lied. Am I that gullible?"

"Darling, I am so sorry, what happened?"

"People say love is blind, and I came to agree with it. There were signs, but I ignored them. There were unexplained absences, until I found out he had been seeing a girl from his hometown for a while. I am so angry and hurt."

"My darling daughter, you don't deserve this, I'll do anything to help you mend your little heart."

"Thank you, Mom, I was thinking you are spending much time alone in the house, it has been too long since we did anything special together. Your life has always been about others."

"I am alright now, Suzy, don't worry about me."

"No, you are not, Mom, I see you are so sad. And, I am not happy either, we need a distraction, a vacation away from here.

What about a girls trip? Tell me a place that you want to go and we'll go together."

"Oh, Suzy, I don't want to go anywhere, I like to be at home."

"Not really, there was a time, since I was very young that you wanted to go to North Carolina, the Outer Banks, remember? You asked Dad, he never made the time for it..."

"Yes, I thought that was a very nice place, like a postcard kind of place."

"To the North Carolina beaches we are going! I am taking you inside that postcard. Let's heal our broken hearts together!"

I broke into tears, embraced my daughter.

"Mom, I just want to see you happy. I love you, Mommy!"

"I love you, Suzy, I want you to be happy too, let's do this."

For my daughter to mend her heart, I forgot mine. I put on my best face, prepared my summer clothes and to the North Carolina shore we went. That was a special treat, I hadn't been away in many years...

We had delightful times, saw the most amazing views of the ocean breaking against the sand, bringing in beautiful shells, breathing the most pure air, but most of all feeling that my daughter cared and loved me enough to share with me that magical experience.

Not far from the bed and breakfast where we were staying, there was a place like a peninsula going out into the water. From that point, playfully, Suzy pointed to the horizon:

"Look, Mom, right there after that line in the horizon there is another continent!"

"Maybe this is as close as I would get... I never traveled abroad. It's good to know it's not far away..."

We laughed, we were relaxing and having fun!

On one of the last nights in the Outer Banks we looked for a new place to see the sunset. There was a promontory over a rocky beach, with a small house on top.

Suzy suggested we go up on the trail. Slowly, and feeling happy that I still could climb, I went up with her.

"With so many beautiful houses in this area who is the lucky one that owns such a lovely cottage? Imagine what a view they have every single day!"

We didn't get too close, there was smoke coming out of the chimney.

"It's summer, that might be an old wood burning stove."

Suzy and I sat on some boulders away from the house, to avoid trespassing. I kept looking back, making a mental picture of the house, and I saw a lady at the door, looking in our direction.

"Suzy, maybe we should go away, there is a lady looking at us."

As we got up, the lady came in our direction, stopped, and spoke.

"You don't have to go, but what are you doing here?"

"I am sorry, we didn't mean to trespass, my daughter and I just wanted to admire the sunset. It's a beautiful view."

The woman looked at me with the most calm expression and beautiful blue eyes. She smiled.

"Enjoy the sunset, and when you are ready to go, come around the house and take a trail that leads to stairs to a parking area. Do not go down on the rocks, especially in the dark, you might get hurt."

"Thank you, you are very kind."

The woman went back into the house.

"Suzy, did you see what a beautiful face? I know she is an old lady, but what a serene expression! With that white lacy shawl over her head and shoulders, she looks like a Madonna!"

I was intrigued.

In that moment I felt a rush of inspiration, thinking of the impression the woman made, and looking at the distance to the endless ocean and the sun going to sleep between the dark clouds of the night, it was a touching experience of pure beauty.

We returned to Virginia feeling rejuvenated, with a lighter soul.

I couldn't wait to start writing my new story, and during the long ride back home I was silent, letting the inspiration flow.

"Mom, you are so quiet. What are you thinking?"

"Oh, Suzy, my brain is spinning, I have a new story brewing here."

"Great! I can't wait to hear it."

"When we get home! The impressions of the Outer Banks are still fresh in me. Thank you, Suzy, for a wonderful time!"

As soon as we got home I wrote down my idea, very quickly. The next morning I told Suzy I was ready to give her the outline.

"I will call it 'The Madonna at Sunset.'

Once upon a time there was a little girl named Ingrid, who at age five was brought to America by her Norwegian mother Britta, a young widow, who came on a work program. On her departure from Norway Britta's mother gave her a white lace shawl, a family heirloom, that she wore at her wedding. The shawl should be passed on to little Ingrid, in the future.

The shawl had an important part in their lives, Britta wore it over her head and shoulders, in times of celebration as well in despair or angst, and she would feel comforted.

She did not know anyone in America nor did she speak the language. Eventually, she was placed with one of the richest families in North Carolina as a maid.

Britta dreamed of giving her daughter all the opportunities for a better life, breaking their cycle of poverty. Young Ingrid grew up with other ambitions, she was happy living in the servants' quarters and playing with the family's children, feeling like she was one of them.

As a young woman she fell in love with the family's second son, Casper, a dashing young man, who apparently reattributed her feelings, and they had a passionate love affair...

From then on she wrote her love story, in poetic letters, and kept them in a pink satin lined trunk. Oh, those letters, so romantic!"

"Are you going to write the letters too, Mom?"

"Yes, Suzy, a few of them. It will be a challenge for me, I am not that romantic, but it is worth the effort... Because there will be a twist!"

"Oh, can you tell me now?"

"Complying with his family tradition Casper left for Oxford, England, like his older brother had done before. He left without saying, 'I'll see you again, someday.'

Ingrid's heart was broken to the point that she gave up living a full life pursuing other interests or relationships. She remained working in the house, letting her youth go by...

Before her death, Britta gave Ingrid the shawl, placing it over her daughter's shoulders she said, 'It will comfort you, it will be your companion for all the unfortunate and also happy times.'

Ingrid was assigned the care of the elderly grandparents, and formed a bond with Old Grandpa, who would take her along wherever he would go. He liked to fish and had a little cottage built on a rocky area, high above the ocean. There together they would spend hours, days, contemplating the vast water.

Ingrid loved that place, and looking at the horizon she would imagine a transatlantic bringing her beloved back to her...

Casper did not return and never gave any thought about her. He married a well-to-do English girl, had a family, and become one of the most renowned and trusted lawyers.

For years, in her obsessive love, Ingrid spent her spare time writing letters of an imaginary life with Casper. Her writings were so profound that she felt the emotions in them contained, and believed they were true. She felt happy and fulfilled.

At a very old age Grandpa died, and he left the cottage to Ingrid, as a gift for all the kind work and company she had offered him.

Ingrid retired and went to live in the cottage alone for a reclusive and quiet life. Among her few belongings she brought along her precious shawl and the box with all her letters.

It was then in solitude that she realized she had lived a delusion, and finally faced reality.

As a ritual, every afternoon she would come out, rain or shine, cold or warm, gaze at the horizon, sometimes with beautiful sunsets, others covered by gray clouds, and would throw one letter into the high tide waves breaking against the rocks, saying:

'*It was nothing but a dream...*'

As she performed that ritual she was filled with serenity. The frayed, discolored shawl over her head and shoulders was the only witness of her acceptance of a life not lived.

Ingrid planned that on the day when she would discard the last letter and see it dissolving into the water, she would come back into the house, would lay on her small bed, and covered by her shawl she would peacefully fall asleep, the eternal sleep."

"Mom, this is so sad! And creepy! Was she sick?"

"Yes, I still have a lot of research to do, only a person with a mental issue could live an entire delusional life and forego everything else. For Ingrid that was better than facing the reality that she didn't have what she mostly desired."

"I like this story, Mom. It's nothing like you created before. Go for it!"

In the beginning of November when the golden leaves were falling, and there was still a warmness in the air, I took the three hour trip to visit Rebekah.

I had called her and wrote to her several times, but that was the first time I was seeing her after the last day in the court house.

The charming woman was gone. Rebekah was now looking older and frail.

"It's the food," she said, "This is what bologna sandwiches for lunch do to you. I don't eat healthy anymore. Goodbye, sushi and salmon, a glass of white wine or fresh smoothies… Those little pleasures mean so much more after we lose them. The ironic thing is that we are allowed to watch TV but most of the time it is on a food channel… Our mouths water." She laughed.

"Other than that, how are you really feeling, Rebekah?"

"I am feeling motivated to paint, and I requested a meeting with my warden to discuss it. But he only allowed me to draw with pencils, nothing else, with that sparse material I'm teaching interested inmates to draw beautiful views.

I want to send them to my son and my best friend, you. The two people in the world that have an interest in me or my art."

"That's wonderful, Rebekah, you have something fun to do."

"Thank you for the North Carolina pictures, Ellen, I enjoyed them, I am saving them, I'll paint some of those views that my eyes would never see."

"Maybe you will, someday. Has Patrick been in touch with you, Rebekah?"

"Yes, he has written a few times, he is thinking of selling the house."

"I know, he spoke to me and told me that he would come soon to get some of the furniture and your paintings, I can help him find a realtor."

"He can do anything he wants, it's his house now. Please, don't let him come to see me. I would love to see my son, but I don't want him to remember me this way. I'm looking so old now. I still want my son to remember me like I was before, when I was younger, healthier."

"Rebekah, I never saw you this way, there is a calmness to you, a serene look in your eyes. You look at peace."

"This is acceptance, I accept my new life condition. This is where I am supposed to be."

"Don't lose hope, Rebekah! One day you will be back to a better life. I miss you, now I talk to you in my writings."

"Are you writing about me, Ellen?"

"I am, it took me a while, next time I come I'll bring you a draft. "

"How are you making me look, like a villain?"

"No, like a human! A human being!"

"Ellen, something I never told you, contrary to your meek and timid demeanor, your writing is imaginative, and you have the guts to put it out there, you are bold!"

"Thank you, Rebekah, I never saw myself as bold, I always lived in the background, not to be noticed..."

I left feeling that I had encountered another person, a humble soul on the firm path to finding peace.

'Blessed is he whose transgression is forgiven, whose sin is covered.'
Psalm 32:1

Patrick came with a moving van. This time he brought his daughter Selena, a beautiful and lively fifteen-year-old girl. I thought I was looking at Rebekah's younger version.

I helped Patrick dispose of many items, and introduced him to a neighbor who owns an antique store on Main Street that took some pieces of furniture, silver and porcelain objects. He packed a few items to take to his home in Atlanta.

Selena was enthralled by the things her grandmother had left, mostly by her paintings and all the accessories, paint, brushes, canvasses, stands, she took everything, saying that like her grandmother she loves to paint!

Oh, Rebekah would love to hear that! I will tell her.

Patrick put the house on the market, didn't take long to be sold. Soon a new couple moved in.

I was melancholic, there was a day years ago, when an elegant lady moved in... Rebekah! I couldn't ever imagine how much she would impact my quiet life.

The first time I saw the new neighbors outside I introduced myself. His wife was standing a little behind him and only smiled. The man responded, "I am Will. How long have you lived here?"

"About sixteen years."

"In that case you might know everything about the previous owner of my house. Did you speak to her?"

"Yes, I did, I do. We are friends."

He frowned, I could see the look of disapproval on his face.

"Someone told me she is in prison. She killed her husband, is that true? If I had known before I would not have moved here."

"No, she didn't, you can find any information online, it's public record."

He turned around, holding his wife's arm to walk into their house. "We have to go."

I knew at that moment those neighbors would never speak to me again. I didn't care about what they thought of me being friends with 'a criminal.'

I felt a little pride for standing up for Rebekah, I was not ashamed of saying she was my friend. I think she was right... I am getting bolder displaying my feelings or thoughts.

In the beginning of the New Year, on a quiet winter day, I received a call from Logan. Since the day Rebekah went to prison I haven't spoken to him.

"Ellen, I am coming out of a hard time, I lost my wife, my dear companion and mother of my children was gone a month ago. She was seriously ill for a while…"

"I'm sorry for your loss, Logan, are you with your family?"

"Yes, they keep me going, we are united on this. Lately I have been thinking of Rebekah, have you seen her?"

"Yes, I saw her last November. She was well."

"Maybe I'll come to visit her, I have plenty of time now, I am retired."

"She said she doesn't want anyone to see her, not even Patrick, she doesn't feel that she looks her best…"

"I don't mind, I am old too, and right now very beaten up."

"I suggest you write to her, Logan. She loves letters and pictures. Maybe you'll send her a nice picture of where you live, she likes to use them as inspiration for her drawings. There are no beautiful views where she is."

"Thanks for the suggestion, Ellen. I'll do that."

"Just remember, don't write anything confidential. They censor the letters in prison."

"I'll keep that in mind. May I ask you, has Patrick spoken to you?"

"As a matter of fact, we have."

"Did he say anything about me?"

"No, Logan, he did not."

"Maybe he never will, but I am open to him."

"Perhaps you need to take the first step."

"I'll take your advice, Ellen. It is nice to talk to you. I will call some other time…"

I didn't feel comfortable talking to Logan, he was someone that I didn't want to maintain contact with. I'll make our conversation shorter if he calls again.

That made me think of how life is disconnected, why people that should be together are separated by misunderstandings, by distance, or time, or death…

I imagined Rebekah in that colorless, sad place, Logan up in snowy Colorado, and their son, somewhere else. They don't have each other. They are all alone.

Something happened to Nicholas. He was excited!
"Isn't it amazing, Mom? When I least expected it there he was. Damian has transferred from New York to be with me in DC."

He brought his boyfriend home to meet me.
Damian had a Scandinavian look and pleasant manners. My first impression of him was of someone that was trying hard to impress, but I was not!
I thought he was older and much more experienced than Nicholas, and the one in charge of their relationship, he expressed they were committed to be together for the long run…
Nicholas looked at Damian with admiration. My son was being led by his emotions, he was naïve, and I hoped he knew what he was doing.
I was uncomfortable and doubtful, it was hard seeing my son embarking on a life opposite from my beliefs and from what I envisioned his life would be, but despite that, I respect his choices and accept him for who he is.
I concealed my feelings.

On a happy note, after being alone for almost a year Suzy met a new man and things are really going well with her new boyfriend.
Russell is a mature, interesting man in his mid-thirties. He came from Australia for an internship in public health and stayed at the NIH as a researcher. Like Suzy he also lives in Silver Spring.
My daughter is in love, and I pray for her happiness!

Many times I walk around with Goldie, together we sit under the shade of the tree in the play area, where I reminisce about my friend, when we sat there with our pads in hand, me writing and Rebekah drawing, talking, laughing and living.
Those times are getting lost in the past…

The neighborhood continues changing. The couple next door moved out of state, the young couple at the right had a baby girl, little Michelle, cute as can be, almost two years old, already practicing with her little three-wheeler on the quiet street.

Phil's wife Lena had to go to an assisted living facility. Incredible as it may seem I hardly saw her. Phil couldn't take care of her anymore. He is alone now, always out walking the dogs and engaging in conversations with everyone he sees around.

We had made an agreement about Goldie, we share custody. With that I see him more often than I want to. He is a talker and he likes to bring news about the neighbors. He irritates me sometimes, asking questions about Rebekah, but I feel sorry for him, another lonely man.

I know what it is like to lose a spouse, sometimes I think of Craig, the way we were, not really close, but I wish I still could see him around, living his life his own way…

Rebekah has been in prison for two years, I visit her twice a year, in the spring and the fall. The last time I saw her I brought a proof of my new book, her story. She was delighted!

"Ellen, did you make a true record of my life as I told you? Are you going to publish it?"

"No, and yes. I needed to write to release my feelings! Most of all I wanted to make a true record of your life, of what you went through, of your qualities, and let go of the negative. I wrote your life story as you told me, and as I saw it."

"I thank you for that, Ellen. I imagined it was unpleasant to you. Now it will be all out in the open and my soul will rest in peace, free of secrets."

"Do you believe in the soul now?"

"I do, Ellen, here I have much time to think about the purpose of life, what comes next after we leave…"

"Well, I have a surprise for you, my friend. I was writing until I got to the chapter when 'my Rebekah' as a young woman was on the brink of breaking away from an abusive marriage, I had to stop there, I am not good at biographies.

Many other ideas were growing in my mind and 'her' life took a completely different direction. From that point on my Rebekah's story became the opposite of what you experienced. It's your life the way it should have been!"

"Oh, Ellen, you did that for me? Can you tell me how? I am so curious now."

"I can tell that 'my Rebekah' made different choices, she ran away from the abuser and went back to her family. Her father and brothers protected her against him. She divorced, and eventually the monster went away.

My heroine found a job in a small hospital in Santee, and she gave a new direction to the lives of her younger siblings. She moved close to the hospital, and brought her brother and sister to attend school there.

In that hospital she met a young doctor. They fell in love, but like everything in life there were challenges, difficulties, but there was much happiness and love.

They married, they moved to a big city, they had children.

'My Rebekah,' the girl who came from a distant poor area in Appalachia, achieved everything she dreamed and deserved, with grit and determination.

I saw that in you, Rebekah! You are my inspiration."

Rebekah was crying.

"I am being immortalized, the best way possible!"

"Yes, the best way possible. And you'll see 'my Rebekah' going through life together with her best friend, on adventures, unexpected twists and turns, sharing their wisdom and true friendship, in good and bad times, until the end."

"That sounds lovely! Thank you, Ellen, you are an angel on earth. Last time my son called me I told him I have an angel watching over me! Next time I'll talk to him, I will tell him 'my angel' wrote me a book."

"How is Patrick doing, is he communicating with Logan?"

"Logan has called him, they talked, but I don't think they would ever be like father and son. Unfortunately, too much time went by, Patrick is a mature man, he doesn't long for a father."

"Maybe they don't have a bond, but they have a connection. I haven't mentioned, Logan called me a couple of times and said he was open to a relationship with Patrick."

"Have you talked to Logan?"

"I did, but not anymore. He was lonely, started calling me after his wife died. He was asking about you and Patrick. He does have much time on his hands, his older son took over their clinic."

"I can see why Logan would talk to you, Ellen, you are a great friend, and attractive…"

"Rebekah, I couldn't offer him support, anything. Somehow he thought he could vent with me about the past. I told him I am your friend, not his."

"We are old friends, aren't we, Ellen?"

"Yes, we are, old friend!"

'The better part of one's life consists of his friendships.'
Abraham Lincoln

Over the years during our personal visits our conversations have changed, Rebekah always finds a way of bringing up chapters or quotes from the Bible that became significant to her. I feel happy knowing that she found solace and comfort, and her new understanding about spiritual life softens her experience in that place.

Another year went on, Suzy and Russell were talking about getting married! That was not a surprise. I was happy with my future son-in-law, a good man.

"I am looking forward to your wedding, Suzy!"

"It will happen soon, Mom."

Nicholas had a setback, Damian ended their relationship and went back to New York. My son came to share the news, to cry and get some comfort.

I embraced him, I knew his heart was broken but knew he would heal and he would find happiness someday, with the right person and right situation.

"Never, Mom, I think I am always going to be alone!"

"No, Nicky, you'll find your right companion someday."

I felt sad for my son, but those are unavoidable situations that we parents can't protect our children from.

"Mom, I'm thinking I need to make a change in my life."

"I understand, Nicky, take your time, you'll find a new way to fulfill your life."

"You have been alone here for too long, Mom, I have a lot of free time on my hands, I'd like to take you out. I heard of a new place in DC that you might like to visit, The Museum of the Bible."

"The Bible Museum! Yes, I saw it in the paper, it must be very interesting. Are you sure you want to take your mother there?"

"Of course, remember how many times you took me to museums and monuments? Now it's my turn, Mom. It will be good for me too, it will take my mind away…"

Nicholas and I went to the museum on Saturday, and I had the most amazing experience, it was much more than I could ever imagine, the display of Middle Eastern manuscripts, artifacts, mostly from ancient Israel, were stunning. Entire spaces were decorated with the history and archeology of the Old World. It was absolutely fascinating.

Nicky and I spent hours there, we had lunch in the cafeteria, a delicious Middle Eastern meal. On the way out we stopped at the gift shop. I thought it was a very special occasion for me to get a new Bible, mine was falling apart. But Nicky went ahead and got me the best and most beautiful issue, with large font letters, bound in leather. A piece to treasure forever.

"Thank you, my son, for this beautiful and rich experience!"

"Mom, I enjoyed it too, it's an amazing and meaningful display, I would come back here again."

Nicky came home with me and stayed until Sunday. He was feeling more optimistic about his future. I know he is going to be alright.

By the holidays, I was happy to have my family at home, Suzy and Nicky and also Russell joined us. 'Life was back home!' I loved it.

Suzy had two announcements. They set a date, and my daughter and Russell will be marrying next year. We have six months ahead to prepare. The young couple was really excited, and so was I.

Suzy also told us that her company is moving to Potomac next year, therefore she and Russell are planning to buy a house after they are married, probably in Bethesda, close to where he works and making her future commute to Potomac easier and shorter.

How many changes! Next year is going to be exciting!

My neighbor Phil and I have been talking often. He is desperately lonely to the point of getting very clingy. Gently, I needed to tell him that I like my time alone, I am so absorbed in my stories that I spend hours writing and don't see the time go by.

I made the mistake to accept his invitation for a New Year's Eve dinner.

What I didn't expect was that he had other plans, after a special dinner at a local restaurant he wanted me to go to his house for a drink to celebrate midnight.

I gently declined, and he spoke of his real intentions, both of us being alone, we should stay together. He couldn't bear to be in an empty house, to sleep alone in a cold bed, he wanted a companion, and he chose me! He was not talking about love, he was talking about loneliness.

We never spoke of that kind of relationship before. I felt terribly uncomfortable.

"We are friends, just friends, Phil. I am sorry there is no room in my life for this kind of relationship. To tell the truth I am perfectly fine alone."

I understood his need for companionship. For me, I was totally satisfied with our brief talks while walking the dogs. I didn't want or expect anything more than that.

He got frustrated and told me he would not waste his time on me. He had been invited to some other friend's house to toast the new year, he left me at my door. That was the first and last time Phil invited me out.

At home, I did what I always do, alone I prayed in thanks for the year ending, and for peace in the world in the year starting.

I then prayed for all my loved ones in heaven, and thought of Craig...

This end of the year I did not call him to invite him to come to reunite with us for the holidays, like I had done before when he responded he was 'too busy.'

I remembered countless celebrations that I spent alone or with the children while he was at the airport. There was no champagne toast, no midnight kisses, no affection or warmth. How could I miss what I didn't have?

At least Suzy and Nicky were happy celebrating with friends.

They called me to say, 'We love you, Mom, Happy New Year!'

A cold winter rolled by while I spent entire days into the night writing, losing myself in my stories, forgetting about time.

In the spring I visited Rebekah again and told her all about the changes that were coming up for my family.

"What about you, Ellen? Will you be moving to the other side of the Potomac?"

"I haven't thought about it. Eventually I'll leave Sycamore Place, but I have no idea where to, most probably to be closer to Suzy and Nicky. I would like to be always around my children."

"That was also my dream, to be close to Patrick. Maybe someday, when I leave this place. In the meantime I'll be busy working on my drawings with my inmates. The clock goes very slowly around here…"

I told Suzy I was going to send her wedding invitation to her father.

"I don't see why, Mom. It has been years, he never called, not even once, for me he is dead!"

"Suzy, he is your father, you are his only daughter, he should know you are getting married. It will be a great opportunity for him to make it up to you."

After I sent the invitation Craig called me for the first time in five years…

He thanked me and said he was not sure he would come, 'too much time had gone by…'

148

He sent a Hallmark card, 'Congratulations on your Wedding' to Suzy, with a gift check.

She was revolted, she wanted to return the check to him. I convinced her not do so.

"Let it go, and spend the money on your honeymoon, leave it all in Australia!"

As a gift to the newlyweds the groom's father offered them a trip to Australia, where they are going to spend time touring around. Suzy will have the opportunity to meet her new relatives.

Suzy was married on a bright and happy summer day, she made the most beautiful bride. Nicholas gave his sister away.

The couple invited their friends for a glamorous reception in a stylish hotel in downtown DC. Russell's brother came from Australia especially for the event.

I was happy with my growing family, at the same time a little sad because my daughter, now married, will rightfully spend less time with me. I need to adjust to that.

I went to see Rebekah in the fall, again!

She looked depressed.

"It has been almost five years that you are here! Didn't it go by so fast?"

"No, Ellen, time drags, the clock doesn't move as fast as in the outside world. Lately I spend a lot of time in bed, I only get up if I have to or when the guards force us out, for a meal or to work.

In my quiet and still time I relive my past, when I was busy working long shifts at the hospital, when the clock wouldn't turn faster than my feet could catch up with it. That was so long ago... Time is all we have, Ellen, maybe you will write something about this."

"Yes, I think it serves as inspiration. 'Time is all we have...'"

"Ellen, my time is up!"

"What are you saying, Rebekah? Haven't you said your lawyer was going to appeal for you to be released earlier, on parole? That might happen, and you'll start a new life in Atlanta with Patrick and your family."

"The appeal is not going to happen, I deserve to be here until the very end to pay for my debt. But, I don't want to think about this now, I want to enjoy our time together. I look forward to your visits, Ellen, I do appreciate you coming from far away. It is a long drive, it might difficult!"

"To be honest it is a little challenging, but I am happy I still can do it. You are worth it, Rebekah."

"You think I have worth? My dearest friend, when I am not here anymore, remember that I loved life, I loved my son, and I loved you. Don't think of me as a convicted criminal, please."

"Rebekah, I will always think of you as my friend, I will remember how you embraced redemption. You are not going anywhere yet, the gate is closed, but it will open for you one day, you will see the light at the other side."

"The light at the other side. Oh, I had a dream about that! I was walking in the fog in the direction of a high iron gate, I could see there was light at the other side and I wanted to be there, so badly. As I approached, the gate opened and I got out of the fog, I felt a sense of warmth and peace like never before, and woke up. I cried, I was still behind a gate, in my cell..."

"That is all symbolic, Rebekah, it's your sub-conscious wanting to be free, you'll be! Don't let hope defer!"

"Ellen, about 'my story' you wrote, I loved it so much, sometimes I hold my book and imagine myself living inside those pages, I almost believe that was my real life.

My son also loved it, the book made him think better of me. I don't want my image to be tarnished.

Is it wrong to hope that the 'ugly truth' would never be known?"

"The truth is that you opened up your soul, you humbly embraced the way to repentance, you connected to God, He accepted your new truth and forgave you. Have peace of mind, you are free, Rebekah!"

"Beautifully said, I am free! Sounds so good. I need to tell you again, I am profoundly grateful for your friendship and understanding.

Thank you, you are a true friend."

"You are also my dear friend, I miss you, too. I'll come back next spring, until then keep the hope!"

'Be of good courage, and He shall strengthen your heart, all you who hope in the LORD.'
Psalm 31:24

The last months of the year rolled by uneventfully.

Nicholas came home for the holidays. He is content with his life. He has moved into a large apartment with two other friends, he is never alone, having fun and working hard.

Suzy and Russell joined us for the weekend. I love the full house when the 'children' are home!

They had plans to look for a house in Bethesda next year, but Suzy's company postponed the relocation.

The young couple had a proposition. They wanted me to move with them into the new house.

"You are here alone, Mom, makes no sense in being away, we would love to have you close, besides we are planning to start a family and I am sure you would enjoy being with your first grandchild."

"I would for sure, Suzy, and I appreciate your invitation, but I am used to being on my own, I know I am getting older but my health is stable and most of all I want to keep my independence."

Russell spoke:

"Ellen, it's not a matter of getting older, we would like to have you close to us, please consider it, when the time comes we could look for a house big enough for all of us, where you still would maintain your independence."

"Thank you, Russell, it's very thoughtful of you, I'll think about it."

That day Russell mentioned that we should be careful this winter, there was news of a flu, in China, a form of pneumonia caused by an unknown virus.

"We don't know much about it yet, and we are hoping that it doesn't spread like some others before. Anyway be aware of any flu symptoms."

We all thought that Russell, as a medical researcher, was giving us his scientific mind alert.

We didn't think much of it, we were excited starting the new decade.

Welcome 2020!

Nicholas returned to DC to celebrate New Year's with his friends.

Suzy and Russell went back to their lives in Silver Spring.

NINE

The winter started out mild.

Usually, I write for long hours during the quiet cold months, but contemplating a possible future move I decided to reduce my load and started looking through old boxes and containers filled with papers, photos, my children's schoolwork, hundreds of cards that they made for me. I had much to go through.

The story of our lives! It was a trip to the past that brought me many memories, some tears of joy, some others not so joyful.

Memories, memories...

This was a time of letting go of the pain that Craig had caused with his emotional detachment, lack of sensitivity to me and the children that left a hole in our hearts and destroyed what could have been a fulfilled relationship.

I had to finally take responsibility for my part, I had been excessively tolerant. I should have put an end to my unfulfilled marriage long ago... Instead, I held on to the hope that someday he would love us and would become the husband and father that we deserved.

Throughout my marriage he was unreachable, and there was nothing I could do besides telling him how much his coldness was hurting us... Oh, I had cried in vain!

Now, once and for all, I was letting go of my feelings towards Craig. Nothing would remain in my heart, no hurt, no pain, no anger, nothing! This chapter was being closed!

I was compelled to make a testament of faith reiterating my firm belief that what happens in life is what is supposed to happen, whether we like it or not we need to accept it, learn from it, and carry on.

'Be strong and of good courage, do not fear nor be afraid of them; for the Lord your God, He is the One who goes with you. He will not leave you nor forsake you.'
Deuteronomy 31:6

During those months I had frequent conversations with Rebekah. It was not easy to speak to her, I needed to call the Correctional Center in advance to make an appointment for her to be allowed to wait for my call by the phone. It was easier for her to call me collect, any time she could, and she did it often.

I became detached to what was happening around, but Suzy and Russell kept me informed. None of us could ever imagine what was to come, not only to America but to the entire world! It turned our lives upside down. A catastrophe!

In March our state was in a lockdown, businesses, schools, even churches were closed. Not that I attended any, but I thought in a phase like that they were essential for many.

Everything became very hard to handle. The pandemic was a pandemonium!

It was the season of being controlled by fear! All of a sudden we were vulnerable, scared, taking precautions like never before, staying locked in our homes like prisoners, facing the invisible enemy, a deadly microscopic virus.

Out of the blue Craig called me, just when I thought I would not hear from him ever again. I was definitely surprised, shocked, to tell the truth.

Apparently, he was concerned about my health status.

"Craig, I really don't know what to make of this call. Are you alright?"

"I am OK, I am not working, everything is a mess right now."

"Yes, it is."

"Ellen, you haven't called me anymore, are you upset I didn't show up for Suzy's wedding? How is she?"

"Suzy is happy. I was upset then, you didn't give the consideration to your only daughter's wedding, but I let it go."

"After so long I didn't know how I would be received."

"We would have treated you with respect, Craig, like we always did."

"Ellen, I have been thinking…" He paused. "Maybe we'll talk some other time. Keep well."

That was the extent of our conversation. I felt sorry for him, he might have been lonely. I knew that for Craig to take the initiative of calling was an enormous step. He was a man of few words.

In the end, I was frustrated he didn't even ask about Nicholas.

I was mostly worried about my son in DC, always surrounded by different people. He guaranteed he was fine and taking all the precautions necessary to avoid any contamination. I trusted him.

With the imposed lockdown I couldn't go to see Rebekah, she was alright, the disease didn't get to the prison. She joked, 'Not even a virus wanted to be behind those walls…'

I was about to call her again, but she did it first.

"I was thinking of you, Rebekah. I am so pleased you called me. How is everything with you?"

"I'm fine, I want to know about you and your family, Ellen. I know you won't be able to come this spring, I will miss you…"

"I'm sorry, Rebekah, maybe in the summer, as soon as the lockdown is lifted I'll come. We are all fine, my daughter and son are both working from home, Russell is working intensely at his lab.

Luckily, I didn't hear of anyone getting ill in our neighborhood."

"That's good news, you take good care of yourself, Ellen, remember you are high risk, your health and life are very precious."

"I will, I am very quiet here, alone at home, Suzy brings me groceries, she doesn't want me out at all.

What about Patrick and his family, have you spoken to him?"

"Yes, he and the family are all fine. I pray this nightmare will soon be over for all of you.

Ellen, I am at fault with you, I don't think I thanked you enough for bringing God into my life. Without any imposition, you showed me a path to faith and hope, which brought peace to my soul. Thank you, my friend!"

She was emotional, I was too. Feeling rewarded, I did help her find peace, but she also had helped me immensely.

"Oh, Rebekah, your words warm my heart. May the Lord bless you and keep you."

"Until we speak again, my angel friend!"

In the beginning of April Nicholas startled me with a call from New York City. I couldn't believe he was there at that critical time. I was anguished.

He said he was alright, but I had a gut feeling... Nicky was not telling me everything.

In a few days it all changed. Suzy came to stay with me.

"I'll be working from here, Mom. Russell is at the lab around the clock. I'll stay with you until this is over."

"What about Nicky? Look at the news, New York is in such disarray, he shouldn't be there."

My son told me I should not worry. But just days later I tried and tried to reach him, he would not pick up his phone. I panicked.

I was at the point of desperation, more than ever I held on to words of strength and faith.

'The Lord is my rock and my fortress and my deliverer; my God, my strength, in whom I will trust.'
Psalm 18:2

"Calm down, Mom. I need to tell you, Nicky called Russell to say that his friend was sick with the virus, and he was taking him to a hospital. He was going to check himself, too."

"Which friend are you talking about, Suzy? Which hospital did he go to? Now I am really worried."

"Nicky went to see Damian, they had been talking... That's why he called us, Mom, he didn't want to upset you. Russell is trying to locate him. He has resources."

"But, Russell is far from Nicky, how can he help him?"

"Mom, please, I am mostly concerned about your health. You can't get this stressed out."

"My son is far away, and I can't be there for him. Why is he not talking to me?"

My beautiful and gentle son was ill, and I couldn't help him or nurse him back to health, I didn't even know where he was. I needed to overcome the angst and fear.

This was a perfect time to apply what I most believed:

'No evil shall befall you, nor shall any plague come near your dwelling. For He shall give His angels charge over you, to keep you in all your ways.'
Psalm 91:10-11

Russell was in contact with the hospital, he was the bridge between Nicholas, the doctors and us. He was following his progress, and he would be discharged soon.

I trusted Russell, he was my only connection with my son.

Days later my son-in-law told me he was going to New York to bring Nicholas to his house. He would quarantine in Silver Spring for two weeks, before joining me and Suzy.

What a blessing to have a son-in-law like Russell!

On their road trip back to Virginia, I spoke to Nicky on the phone, he was very weak, but on his way to recovery. He was sad, crying, his friend Damian didn't survive...

"He asked for my help, Mom, and I went, I still loved him."

"I am very sorry, son. I can't wait for you to be home, I will help you heal."

After two weeks, Nicky came to our house, emaciated, brokenhearted, but determined to recover soon.

Hugging him he cried like a little boy, I cried too.

'Thank you, Lord!' My 'baby boy' was home, I could nurse him back to health. I could try to ease his pain, and couldn't thank Russell enough for bringing my son back to me.

"You are a true son! I am happy Suzy married the best man ever!"

The tragic events continued happening all over.

Spring was not a happy one, we were locked in our houses. Suzy and Russell were still apart.

At summer's arrival, Suzy finally went back to her home to be with her husband.

As the days got warmer, that motivated me to spend more time walking outside, and many times I brought Nicky along.

Even if he was not fully recovered, he resumed working remotely.

"Mom, do you mind that I am staying with you longer than expected?"

"Absolutely not, son, this is your home too! On the contrary, I love your company, most of all I want to see you well."

"I do love to be here too, Mom. I don't feel like being in DC anymore with all the election turmoil, Washington is a boiling pot. I don't know if I ever want to go back."

"Nicky, you have all the space in the master bedroom, make it your own. This is your home. I am happy you are here until this nightmare is over."

During the lockdown I spoke to Rebekah several times.

"Sorry I neglected you, Rebekah, things have been hectic. Suzy was here for a long time, just went back to her life, Nicholas is still recovering. I am well, only tired."

"Your son will be alright, he is young and strong. I am happy he is there, you are the best company."

"What have you been doing, Rebekah? Is there any activity allowed?"

"Not much, we have to maintain the distance... I pray and pray."

"Rebekah, let's wait for the fall, I hope I will be able to see you, this situation should be over then."

Months after the disease Nicholas sometimes lacked energy. It was a lengthy recovery, but he kept himself busy, spending his days locked in his room, working at his computer, meeting his co-workers and friends online, moving forward.

We had a summer unlike any other, there was chaos, violence, fires, revolt and destruction of private and public property, and unfortunately many deaths. Some in the media called it the 'Summer of Love'!!!

It was a blunt display of lawlessness and disorder, and we heard the words 'woke' and 'cancel culture' quite often.

"What exactly does that mean?" I asked my son. "I have heard in these past few tumultuous years references to 'woke.' Is that a movement?"

"You can say that, Mom! Woke is a slang word now officially added to the dictionary, it means to be awake to sensitive social issues, such as racism or social injustice. But, as claiming victim status some use it as a weapon through acts of intolerance or violence against those perceived as not woke."

"I feel like I have been asleep all this time. When did this start, Nicky?"

"Decades ago, when schools were told not to inject God or morality into education. Children were discipled in secularism (keep God out), humanism (man is his own god), relativism (there are no absolutes) and even atheism. Scary as it is this is my generation!"

"You are brilliant, Nicky, you understand what is happening. How can it be fixed?"

"Standing up, like you do, Mom, for law, for faith, for God, promoting peace and resolution."

"After knowing this I understand the cancel culture better now, being silenced, fired, removed from social media, when what is said is not in accordance to their agenda.

There is a total disregard of the real facts, and no respect for free speech. Different ideas or opinions are not debated or heard, they are simply cancelled, erased!

How in the world will we ever achieve peace if we can't intelligently and respectfully discuss our opinions or beliefs?"

I found myself more and more invested in what was happening. Nicky and I were having long conversations about the situation in the nation and other worldwide events, things were dramatically changing everywhere.

"What's happening to our country, to our planet? America has become a nation of conformists. In many ways it is disrespectful of God's governing principals. Men are doing barbaric things to each other because they forgo God's laws."

In the midst of the confusion of the post-election disarray I turned to my old source of information about our Republic. I had read before in my Lincoln book many passages and statements that he made about our nation's core values. I could clearly see that we were distancing ourselves from those principles, the foundation of our magnificent country.

In November 1863, in his Gettysburg Address, Lincoln said:

'... That this nation, under God, shall have a new birth of freedom, and that government of the people, by the people, for the people, shall not perish from the earth.'

He also stated:

'My concern is not whether God is on our side; my greatest concern is to be on God's side, for God is always right.'

I discussed with Nicky what I had learned from history, so far.

"I can only stand by God and the Country."

"Mom, you always have an approach based on the spiritual aspect, and you are right about this. Our nation was founded under God, following His principles. I went deep in American history when I was in college and saw this written all over.

160

'In God We Trust' is the theme for our nation, and look at the Founding Fathers, they all expressed that God is about government, freedom and prosperity, it's about protecting people's lives, even if we have to war to achieve peace and justice for all."

"Son, you surprise me! I think you are so right. I am glad you accept my idea that what is happening is caused by a disregard of principles of love for one another, truth and justice."

I started digging deeper into America's history with my son's help. I was amazed by how much he knew, and our conversations got more informative and interesting.

It was not possible to visit Rebekah in the fall, I was upset. An entire tumultuous year went by without seeing her. Anyway, we continued talking. I spoke to her around Thanksgiving.

"Sorry, Rebekah, I couldn't come to see you this year, I couldn't even send you a care package, the Institution didn't allow it."

"I understand, Ellen, I miss you, but I am fine. With all that is happening I have plenty of time to pray in preparation for my departure."

"Departure, Rebekah! Are you being paroled?"

"Yes, into the hands of Heavenly Father, sometime soon I hope! I reached a point of the most profound peace, my heart longs to 'go home'!"

"Rebekah, God will bring you 'home' in His time! You do not have to accelerate the process. Promise me!"

"Don't worry, my friend, I am patient. I feel joy when I think of 'going home'! And, when it happens, please do not cry for me, rejoice, I'll be free! This time let me offer you a prayer that I find timely:

'And God will wipe away every tear from their eyes; there shall be no more death, nor sorrow, nor crying. There shall be no more pain, for the former things have passed away.'
Revelation 21:4

"Goodbye, my angel friend!"

"Goodbye, dear Rebekah. May God bless you and keep you!"

I had tears in my eyes and a knot in my throat.

That conversation left me with a profound feeling…

Suzy was still working remotely in Silver Spring. With the lockdowns her office building did not move to Potomac, everything was on hold, including their plans to buy a house. She was frustrated, things were not moving…

I just kept telling my daughter, "This shall pass."

Exactly fourteen days after I had spoken to Rebekah, Patrick called me.

"Ellen, I have sad news. I got a call from the Penitentiary earlier this morning, my mother has passed away."

I choked. Then a calm descended on me.

"I'm very sorry, Patrick. What happened to Rebekah, was it the virus?"

"No, they said it was cardiac arrest. It was very sudden. You are the first I am notifying, you were her best friend, the only one who cared to visit her. Did you see anything happening to her when you saw her last?"

"Yes, it was Thanksgiving last year, she said she dreamed of 'seeing the light at the other side of the gate,' it looked like she was saying at the other side of the prison gate in the future after her release, but I knew exactly what she meant.

Then when we spoke throughout the year she often would repeat that her time was up. Also, on our last call she mentioned she was ready to 'go home.' She was prepared, Patrick, your mother went to the light, she is free!"

He was crying.

"I didn't love my mother enough, I was waiting to make it up to her when she was out. Now I have no chance to do it." He took a deep breath.

"The prison warden offered the option of sending me her ashes. What do you think she wanted, Ellen, did she ever mention to you?"

"No, she never discussed what she wanted after… But I know for certain your mother wanted to be with you. For all her life, she wanted to be close to you!"

"I know! I'll bring her ashes home, my family and I will honor her."

"I'm sure your mother would be blessing you for that, Patrick!"

"Ellen, have you talked to Logan lately? Are you going to inform him?"

"No, I haven't spoken to Logan. What about you?"

"I really don't feel like talking to him. To be honest, once in a while we communicate, but I never felt I wanted to get close to him. He is a friendly stranger to me. I don't want to keep the conversation going, but if he calls me one of these days, I'll let him know."

"You are right, Patrick, sometimes it's just too late when someone comes into our lives, not the right time."

After talking to Patrick, I reflected about Rebekah and the sorrow of loved ones being separated by events in life as well as by death. But I had the comfort to know that she was prepared to go on.

We became the best of friends, we shared years of mutual support and empathy. She was the one who motivated me during my illness, and dried my tears when I hurt emotionally by my husband's sudden departure. She trusted me, telling me her most dark secrets, knowing that I would show her compassion, and gave me the chance to support her through her redemption, finding peace.

I will miss her dearly, and our conversations that lasted for ten years. Even when she was 'behind the iron gates' our communication didn't cease.

'Oh, Rebekah, last time we spoke you said goodbye, my angel friend!'

I was profoundly touched and offered her a familiar prayer, the same I said for my loved ones:

'The Lord bless you and keep you;
The Lord make His face shine upon you, and be gracious to
you; The Lord lift up His countenance upon you, and give you
peace.'
Numbers 6:24-26

My son comforted me.

"Her sentence has ended, Mom, and she knew you were a great friend, you didn't desert her even when she was convicted."

"She was also a great friend to me! I feel all is right, she found eternal peace."

I called my daughter to tell her, "Rebekah has 'gone home,' she is free! I feel sorry for Patrick, he didn't have the time to be close to his mother!"

Gladly, Suzy and Russell came for Christmas, after so long we were reunited for two days. We agreed not to talk about the distress around us, we made it a time for peace. At least between our walls there was unity and harmony.

We had a sweet time, the presence of my children always fills my heart with joy!

After they left, I told Nicky I was happy for him being there with me. He was my soul mate, we had so much in common, we could talk about anything. I was praying for his happiness and his progress in all aspects of his life, every day.

"Mom, your prayers are being answered, there is something I want to share with you, it's very personal. I am going through a process of being true to myself. What I want to say is, Damian was the only relationship I ever had but even before his death I started questioning my sexual orientation.

I do not want to be a confused individual.

Honestly, I do not know what led me to this. Was it DNA? A physical dysfunction? Emotional? Psychological? Was it because I was a little more sensitive than the other boys? Or was it the lack of a father's love and example? I truly have no idea what was the determining factor or factors for me being this way. But I am working on it."

"I wish I could help you on that, Nicky. However, you do have my support."

"Yes, I know. Sorry I have something to tell you about Dad. When I was young many times he mocked me or criticized the way I talked, walked, 'like a girl.' He was cruel and a coward, he always did that when you were not around. I am sure he had an impact on me."

164

I was heartbroken.

"I am so sorry, Nicky, why did you never tell me? Oh, I would have jumped on him like a lioness, and that marriage would have been over long, long ago."

"That's what I feared. I didn't want to cause any turmoil. I saw your struggle to keep the family together..."

"Thank you for confiding in me, son. Makes me ill to think your father was the only man I loved, now I only pity him!"

"As far as I am concerned, he didn't deserve you, Mom."

"Now it is all about you, Nicky. What are you thinking of doing?"

"I found a doctor to help me regain my strength and fully recover my health, in the process I will have all sorts of physical tests to see if anything else is wrong with me, and if it can be fixed or not. I'm also open to speak to a psychologist or psychiatrist specialized in gender issues.

I am searching for an answer to define myself. When we know who we really are, we should not be in conflict, don't you think?"

"I think you are right, and I support you on your quest."

"Mom, thank you for not being judgmental, and for loving me just the way I am."

"It's a given, son, I love you unconditionally and forever."

That conversation made me feel really good. Nicky was taking charge of himself physically and emotionally. I did not have to worry about him, I only prayed for his happiness and fulfillment.

I thought I needed to tell him that during many years I thought his father had an issue, he lacked passion, and the wall that he put between us in my opinion was to protect himself and his image... Was I just making excuses for Craig's lack of feelings? Was there a genetic reason for Nicky to be the way he is? It would be fair to tell him another time, today we already had a charged conversation about his father.

On the last day of the year, almost a year after his first call, Craig called me. 'Oh, no!'

"Just to wish you a Healthy New Year, Ellen. How are you?"

"I am fine, what about you, Craig?"

"I am OK. I am thinking about moving to a new community for retired folks by a golf course, they have great homes with beautiful views. Would you like to see it? Maybe after the winter when things go back to normal."

He never disclosed so much before in one sentence. I was flabbergasted.

"No, Craig, I don't know when or if things will be back to 'normal,' and you don't need me to decide what is best for you."

"What I mean is that maybe you would like to move here. I am alone, you are alone..."

"I am not alone, I have Nicholas and Suzy, and I always want to be close to my children. Craig, I don't know why you'd think I would move to be with you. Is that your intent?"

"Well, Ellen, we are still married."

"Only on paper, and I am ready to finalize it. Our marriage was over long before you left... For my part, I let you go, Craig, but, remember if some day you decide to initiate communication with your son and daughter, the door is open."

"I see, too much time has gone by... I am sorry, Ellen."

"I wish you well, Craig, and good luck in your new community."

My son was close by.

I was a little distressed. He embraced me.

"I feel sorry for Craig, he is old and lonely. He never reached out to me this way. But I have to be true to myself, I was unhappy all my life at his side, it's too late! And I didn't even have the energy to discuss the past...

Recently, I came to the realization that he did me a favor when he left, he released me from that agonizing situation."

"Mom, you did right to him, you have nothing to regret."

I was anxious for the end of this most difficult and eventful year. This new decade has started out harsh, and we could only pray and hope that in the year to come we will accomplish health, peace, and resolution. Whatever may come our way, in faith, we will stand!

In 2021 the political and social unrest, and the doom and gloom of the epidemic continued.

It was a time for humanity to rise up above the dark circumstances, calamities and losses, and turn to work, faith and hope. Unfortunately, it did not happen that way.

I was compelled to join others who like me were in search of the truth, and connected to a daily prayer group of two hundred thousand intercessors, fighting for the same purpose and intention: Healing!

Healing of political issues, and also of the people, tired and discouraged in the face of hard life conditions after a long, challenging year...

Praying together we become stronger!

'If My people, who are called by My name will humble themselves, and pray and seek My face, and turn from their wicked ways, then I will hear from heaven, and will forgive their sin and heal their land.'
2 Chronicles 7:14

For the first time I made the connection between the laws of government with the book that has made the most impact: the Bible. The Old Testament's major theme was of two kingdoms, good and evil, acting through men hungry for power, warring for control of the land and the people!

'That which is has already been, and what is to be has already been; and God requires an account of what is past.'
Ecclesiastes 3:15

It was a parallel of what is happening in our world now, it has already happened in another era. History keeps repeating itself, it has been written thousands of years ago. Fascinating!

Motivated to continue studying I connected with evangelical teachings to learn about prophetic interpretations of ancient and current events in the world, and immediately found a biblical link between love and loyalty to the country.

'Declaring the end from the beginning, and from ancient times things that are not yet done, saying, 'My counsel shall stand.''
Isaiah 46:10

I found a Pastor in Nashville who I loved to listen to. He was teaching us much about 'The Word,' and I decided to start watching his Sunday services, too. Couldn't wait to tell my son about it.

Once again Nicholas was right about 'God is government!' That's how our nation was founded, but we have been complacent, walking away from it. We need to return to our fundamental principles.

Since the very beginning America was proclaimed to be:

'You are the light of the world. A city that is set on a hill cannot be hidden.'
Matthew 5:14

In 1607, when Robert Hunt landed at Cape Henry he planted a cross and declared:

'From these shores the Gospel shall go forth to not only this New World but to the entire world.'

Americans with a pioneer spirit shall be unwilling to settle for things as they are, they will help us find the old road back to our roots.

I also continued dedicating time learning more about our Founding Fathers, the Declaration of Independence, and the Constitution.

Our nation's government, composed of three branches; judicial, legislative and executive, was based on the Scriptures:

'For the Lord is our Judge, the Lord is our Lawgiver, the Lord is our King; He will save us.'
Isaiah 33:22

Oh, I wish I could share all of that with my friend! Rebekah was open minded, for all I knew she liked to be well informed.

Sitting under our tree, we had conversations about events in our country and in the world that continued through the time even when she was 'behind the iron gate' by phone or letters.

Out of Rebekah's mouth I never heard a biased word towards people with whom she didn't share the same beliefs. We openly discussed our points of view, and respected each other's opinions, although we were very different.

I missed her…

Many times, from my window I glanced at her former house across the street, and remembered the first time I saw her coming to greet me. She was friendly and warm. I was impressed, she was dressed elegantly in black slacks and a white shirt, wearing a pearl necklace, didn't seem that was her moving day at all.

From that day on, every time I saw her she had her one strand pearl necklace on. She said it was the first gift Colton had given to her, and she would never take it off! But there came a day when she was forced to leave it behind. Oh, Rebekah…

I had no other friends in the neighborhood to talk to anymore. Some older residents had moved away, including Phil, he took Goldie, and never said goodbye. There were a few left, but they seemed judgmental, since Rebekah went to prison they gave me a cold shoulder, some were even hostile. I knew it was because I continued supporting her.

Well, they were not really my friends.

When Nicholas had time we discussed our ideas and findings. I felt an enormous satisfaction for sharing my most inner convictions with him, and gladly was surprised by how much we thought alike.

"Nicky, I have found a Pastor in Nashville, Tennessee who I am following online. Imagine me, I never attended any church, maybe because of my bad experience in childhood. But this is different, it's educational and interesting, and I appreciate their choir. Beautiful music!"

169

"Funny that you mention Nashville, Mom. Lately, I reconnected to my friend Jason from college. We worked together in the drama club. He lives in Nashville, his hometown."

"Really! I remember him. Don't take it the wrong way, Nicky, is Jason…"

"No, no, I know what you are thinking, Mom. Jason is a straight man, he married right after college, has two children. We were good friends.

His father went into the business of recording Gospel music, and eventually built a studio that produces heroic and inspirational movies."

"I am glad, Nicky, it is always good to reconnect with old friends."

Misleading is a nice word to describe some of the mainstream news and social media. The misinformation was appalling. I stopped watching them, I remained fully aware of the media's attempt to distract us with fear and distortions.

Many citizens will be devastated and angry when things are unveiled, and they will realize they were deceived.

I needed to stay informed and spent countless hours researching and reading reports from several sources, including Christian networks, comparing information with public written records or videos. I wanted to know the facts, not others' biased opinions.

It became clear to the patriotic community that unruly governmental decisions were being made, jobs and business continued being lost, stirring a spirit of revolt and division among many seeing their most basic rights being taken away.

What happened to freedom of speech? Isn't that constitutional?

That made me interested in the Constitution even further.

My bright son took upon himself the role of my 'history teacher,' providing me printouts and information. He brought to my attention:

"Mom, I see why you feel this way, America is rooted in the Word of God, it is impressed all over, in every document since our foundation, in every national hymn. The framers of our Constitution would not recognize the America that they established. George Washington wrote:

'Of all the dispositions and habits which lead to political prosperity, religion and morality are indispensable supports. It is impossible to rightly govern the world without God and the Bible.'

John Quincy Adams added:

'The highest glory of the American Revolution was this: it connected in one indissoluble bond the principles of civil government with the principles of Christianity.'

The Battle Hymn of The Republic can be sung as a prayer:

'Mine eyes have seen the glory of the coming of the Lord
He is trampling out the vintage where the grapes of wrath are stored
He have loosed the faithful lightening of his terrible swift sword
His truth is marching on!'

And, in God Bless America:

'God bless America, land that I love
Stand beside her and guide her
Through the night with the light from above.'

God is also present in the National Anthem:

'Then conquer we must, when our cause is just,
And this be our motto – In God is our Trust –
And the star-spangled-banner in triumph shall wave
Over the land of the free and the home of the brave.'

Eventually, Nicholas joined me on one or another Sunday for the Evangelical church service. He appreciated it, and I appreciated even more sharing that time with him, learning together something new and inspiring.

There was oppression over the Christian faith and values, even in the House of Representatives, recorded in forum, they said *'God has nothing to do with this house'* for all to see the display of their humanism, which is a religion gearing to 'cancel' the Christian faith and believers.

Really? Did they forget that our Declaration of Independence states clearly that 'God is our Creator, Lawmaker, Judge and Protector?' How can they publicly disregard our most basic principles? They certainly have the right to be non-believers, but do not mock God!

I am not a historian or qualified to debate about it, I am only a concerned citizen who loves our country. There is no doubt this dark period is going down in history.

The new government was changing the character of our country, and it was frightening to see the direction it was taking. This has been happening for a while, we just had been oblivious to it. Now the clear signs of socialism and secularism were evident: silencing, erasing voices and opinions contrary to the opposition was a major one. Also imposing restrictions and mandates, it was equal to a loss of our freedom! It was happening worldwide! The globalism philosophy was taking over.

Globalism! Some people had been strategically placed in government positions of power, and they were changing the world! The way we live, the way we think, the way we worship. What a scary reality!

My passion for truth and justice was ignited. I put my stories on hold. The values of freedom, truth and justice never change, they are forever. We need to stay the course: Stand!

In the midst of all of this, my family gave me a beautiful day to celebrate my sixtieth birthday! A milestone for which I am grateful, considering that it has been a decade since the MS diagnosis, I am still active and looking forward to the new phase of my life.

According to my son and daughter age doesn't matter. I am more vibrant than ever, I was transformed from a docile person into a passionate defender of truth!

As Abraham Lincoln said:

'In the end it's not the years in your life that counts. It's the life in your years.'

I came across a blog of patriots saying, 'United we stand! We will not waver in this important time.'

They divulged this Lincoln quote that resonated with me:

'America will not be destroyed from the outside. If we falter and lose our freedom, it will be because we destroyed ourselves.'

I couldn't resist and started contributing to that site weekly, with quotes from Lincoln's speeches, my lifelong inspiration!

I have learned about many others in government, civilians and military, who loved our country and sacrificed even their own lives, but for me Lincoln was still above all. The one who stood up, and put an end to America's shameful sin – slavery.

We need men like Abraham Lincoln, like Martin Luther King Jr. who fought and died for unity, equality and freedom for all!

Where are those men?

Under the guidance of the Pastor, we found teachings, acts of mercy, and miracles that gave us faith that we would come out of the current state.

We became aware that a new spiritual consciousness and enlightenment were emerging. A great spiritual awakening was coming.

Our horizons expanded further, and we verified that what was happening to America was happening worldwide! There was a universal hunger for righteousness and justice.

Nicky showed me in the Preambles to the Constitutions of the fifty states, God or Almighty God was included in all.

"From the 1700's to the 1900's, since the three first states, Pennsylvania, Maryland and Virginia in 1776, until the last one, Hawaii in 1959, they made a reference to God! How can anyone, in government or not, profess otherwise?"

Like many others, I refused to yield to anxiety, I not only prayed, I took action, signing petitions, calling local government officials.

I became emboldened and posted an 1863 Proclamation of Prayer from Abraham Lincoln, as relevant today as it was 150 years ago.

'We have the recipients of the choicest bounties of Heaven. We have been preserved, these many years, in peace and prosperity. We have grown in numbers, wealth and power, as no other nation has ever grown. But we have forgotten God. We have forgotten the gracious hand which preserved us in peace, and multiplied and enriched as strengthened us; and we have vainly imagined, in the deceitfulness of our hearts, that all these blessings were produced by some superior wisdom and virtue of our own. Intoxicated with unbroken success, we have become too self-sufficient to feel the necessity of redeeming and preserving grace, too proud to pray to the God that made us.'

Although many Patriots were not Christians, they validated it. Some of them made comments like 'a true Patriot stands for transparency, truth and justice.'

Things heated up further!
It became clear that we were in the middle of a spiritual battle among good and evil, and we needed to restore our true purpose and calling.

There were times during the hot summer that things looked lost, the obstacles to achieve a just resolution seemed immensurable, and many started feeling down, hope was deferred, but we continued lifting one another up with our weapons: faith and encouraging words.

The Biblical lessons nurtured me and lifted my spirit in times when I heard something negative. The words of goodwill are eternal and powerful, and through them I stayed the course.

'But those who wait on the Lord shall renew their strength; they shall mount up with wings like eagles, they shall run and not be weary, they shall walk and not faint.'
Isaiah 40:31

The other side was taking outrageous measures to silence us from speaking, and to stop us from digging into claims of irregularities with the last election. If they were so sure there was no evidence of errors or wrongdoing, why do they continuously try to stop anyone from verifying?

It was obvious, they wanted to exercise complete control of America to transform it into a secularist, globalist nation.

Some state legislators, lawyers, patriots were under pressure, some even threats, but courageously they continued pushing forward.

'Arise, Patriots! Protect our freedom!'

The Reagan Freedom Speech in 1964, years before he became president, sheds light on the precarious nature of freedom, relevant now more than ever, and still serves as inspiration:

'Freedom is never more than one generation away from extinction. We didn't pass it on to our children in the bloodstream. The only way they can inherit the freedom we have known is if we fight for it, protect it, defend it, and then hand it to them with the well fought lessons of how they in their lifetime must do the same. And if you and I don't do this, then you and I may well spend our sunset years telling our children and our children's children what it once was like in America when men were free.'

Before all of this happened, I never cared for politics, neither had a party affiliation, as an independent thinker I always loved our country, and believed people were created to be free.

My patriotism grew exponentially, fed by faith in this land, in the heroes of our nation. I continued fervently praying for freedom, truth and justice, knowing with certainty it was coming at the right time.

Truth is like a flowing river, it always runs to the open waters for all to see.

The great Winston Churchill made this statement that no one can deny:

'The truth is incontrovertible. Malice may attack it, ignorance may deride it, but in the end, there it is!'

I was so involved with much going on that I didn't see time go by. I had been stuck in my house for so long that when I went around my neighborhood I didn't recognize some of the new faces. Everything was changing, but my tree, as always, was standing tall and strong, defying time, forces of nature, unrest, sickness. 'Oh, majestic tree!'

When it seemed like we could not be shaken by more bad news, our government relinquished Afghanistan back to the terrorists that took over billions of dollars worth of U.S. military equipment, as well as hundreds of American hostages were left behind.

It was a punch to our hearts that left us feeling vulnerable and disgusted by that debacle. The independent reports were devastating, people were being killed, tortured.

'Lord, have mercy on the innocent people trapped in Afghanistan!'

Nicholas had spent the last months in treatment and he was going through a visible and positive improvement. He had more energy, and advised by his doctors among other medications he was under a closely monitored hormonal treatment. During the initial tests they found a severe deficiency, the treatment also helped with depression, something he didn't realize he was suffering from. He started exercising and showed great disposition overall.

Throughout these past months Nicholas was invested in a new project, and he was finally ready to tell me.

"Mom, there was something missing from my life, authenticity! I decided my career based on the skills that I was proficient in, not on the ones I was talented to work with it. Since high school I had a great interest in theater production. I loved it, it was fulfilling and fun.

During these months Jason discussed his work with me, producing movies and documentaries on world events, and real-life inspirational stories of courage and heroism, promoting the best in humankind.

I asked him to get involved, he gave me the opportunity to work on one project, and it has been a rich experience. He thought we should work together again, like we did in college, and made me an offer to work with him, writing, and producing.

I found my calling, Mom. I really want to do this, therefore I am quitting my job in DC."

"Nicky, I truly believe this is a time of transformation and opportunity on the professional level and spiritual growth as well. There are infinite possibilities, the things you didn't pursue before are now in your reach. I am proud of you, son! Go forward!"

"So, you support me, Mom?"

"Of course, with all my heart! I know how talented you are, you will succeed.

Nicky, I have seen your effort in putting your health back together, and I can see the results. What about the other issue, are you feeling any different?"

"I think the hormonal imbalance had a serious effect on me. But, so far I have no interest whatsoever in any personal relationship, male or female. I still need help to sort it out. I am talking to a specialist, maybe I am one of those individuals who can't form a healthy intimate attachment with anyone... Mom, do you think I am like my father?"

"Nicky, now you made me think! Your father was cold, emotionally detached and incapable of loving. He lacked passion and avoided intimacy, I always believed it was due to his upbringing. I don't know what his real issue was, but I know that you are not like him, you are loving, caring and able to form relationships with us, your family and others.

I applaud you for continuing working on this. Don't give up."

"Mom, I noticed the other day during the Sunday service when the Pastor was addressing homosexuality, you heard it attentively and made no comments. Thank you for giving me space to reflect about it."

"I trust your judgment, son, and I know you will honor your true self."

That night alone in my room I prayed for my son. I do have a bit of sadness knowing that he struggles, there is nothing I can do but to support him. I just want him to be happy.

Rarely do Suzy or Nicky talk about their father. As for me the memories of him are fading away... Sad to realize that he passed through our lives and in the end left a void, an empty space.

Life has been difficult, at times brutal, the struggling economy is destroying the dreams of many, diseases have multiplied and continue taking lives, and unreasonable mandates are stirring anger and disbelief. Not only in our country, but the entire world is filled with unrest.

During this revolting and traumatic time, on this September 11th, the country paid homage to the thousands lost in the 2001 terrorist attack. Twenty years have gone by, and this is with no doubt the most painful tribute.

The pain of millions of Americans is being magnified by the recent events. We prayed for the thousands that lost their lives, and for their families. My heart and the hearts of many hurt, immeasurably. We grieve!

My daughter calls or comes to see me often. She has been upset lately. Russell has not shown much interest in resuming their search for a house, their plan was put on hold again.

Suzy invited me to come with her to see some houses.

"Mom, now in the fall it's a buyer's market, I went on my own and found a large house, it has an entire independent three-room apartment on the ground floor with a separate entrance and windows to the backyard, patio and garden. It's fabulous! Would you like to come and see it?"

"Suzy, if you like the house I'll like it too. But I am not in a hurry, as long as Nicky is here I am not going anywhere. You know what a difficult time your brother has had, he is starting something new, and I have no idea when he is moving out.

Anyway, I am a little puzzled. Why is Russell not motivated to make that decision? Does he really want me to be around? I do not want to be a burden to you or your husband."

"No, Mom. Russell likes you very much and you will be independent. You'll have your own apartment, a floor away from us. Russell just has other things on his mind lately…"

"Do you want to talk about it?"

"Well, he has been distressed about the situation in Australia, these past months he has been in close contact with his family there. Things are happening that he totally disagrees with. As he calls it, 'the government's draconian laws' are destroying lives and progress in the country. Using the Covid situation they have an iron fist over the people, they are having their liberties taken away by law enforcement.

Unvaccinated people are being treated as prisoners. Do you know that they built 'quarantine camps' outside Darwin?"

"No! I know the whole world is a mess, and in many countries people are being pressured, living in fear. It's difficult to find the right news from abroad, there is secrecy and cover-ups."

"Yes, Russell feels the same way, he is devastated, and with the scientific knowledge he has about the virus he believes that prevention and treatment should be done differently and not used as a weapon to demoralize the population. He feels like what is happening is a crime against humanity. He is very angry. I never saw him this way."

"I understand how he feels, I think daily about our own country and I can't stop contributing with words of faith and hope, and most of all believing that justice will be done.

Nevertheless, we can't succumb to it, life goes on, and we need to maintain optimism and carry on with the normal course of our lives, while fighting the hardships."

"That is what I tell Russell, we'll do what we can, in the meantime we continue living, we continue our plans in defiance of what others dictate to us. I believe it is time for us to get our own home, to move on, and start a family. I long to have a family."

"Those are all natural and fair desires. Suzy, I agree we can't lose perspective, life goes on. And, yes, in time everything will fall in the right place."

"I am trying to be understanding, Mom, I had told Russell that I will continue looking, we really need a house, but I am sensible, I am not going to make a rushed decision."

"That's wise. You and Russell have time to find the right home!"

I realized that for the past year and a half I had only two interests, taking care of my son who finally has recovered, and the state of our nation.

Consistently, I spent all my days researching, reading, getting informed, blogging and praying.

'Wait on the Lord; Be of good courage, and He shall strengthen your heart.'
Psalm 27:14

TEN

On the first days of October, Suzy brought me some startling news. She was in tears. Russell decided to take a three-month sabbatical to go to Australia to join his father, brother and other friends, using his scientific research skills to help a community of doctors and health experts in the fight against the government-imposed demands.

"When is he going, Suzy?"

"Now! He already received the approval for his sabbatical, which he requested without discussing with me in advance."

"I understand his passion, but I am shocked, Suzy. Is this an emotional reaction to what is happening in his country or something else? Russell never made decisions based on emotion... I hope that after these three months he will come to his senses and realize that he might be able to help his family and his fellow citizens without leaving this country, where his family is, you!"

"He said he will come to say goodbye to you, Mom, and will explain why he feels compelled to do this, he is being 'called to duty.' I can't make any sense out of it! No matter how he justifies it, I am angry and brokenhearted."

I hugged my daughter.

"Suzy, I understand. This shall pass, darling. I validate your feelings, but despite what is going on don't give up your dreams, faith will see you through. You should know that I am also disappointed about what he is doing to you. It should have been your joint decision!"

"That's what hurts, Mom. His family in Australia is more important to him than me and our marriage…"

In the evening I told Nicky I was terribly upset about how Russell's sudden decision was affecting Suzy.

"Our time together is very precious to me, son, being able to share my feelings and beliefs with you has been absolutely fulfilling, but now we need to embrace Suzy and lift her up. Together, the three of us can overcome anything."

"I agree, and right now with this new unexpected development I am feeling really bad… As I mentioned before, Jason wants me working with him in Nashville. As soon as I can I am flying over there to discuss all the arrangements, see housing, et cetera."

"Nashville! I was expecting that to happen, you need to live your life, son, and it is your right to do so."

"I am sorry, Mom, I need to go on, but I will always be connected to you. But while I am here we will make the best of our time together with my sister.

Remember when I was little you used to read me a story, 'I Love You Forever,' about a mother and her little boy through all the stages of his life, and then later when he was a mature man and his mother an old lady, he took care of her. In the end I used to say, 'I love you forever, Mom, I'll take care of you!'"

"I remember, Nicky, I still have that book with others from your childhood. I used to respond to you, 'From here to eternity my baby you'll be,' I meant it. I will miss you dearly, but I support you wholeheartedly, follow your path."

"Let's make these next few months as soft as possible for Suzy. And, after I move I won't forget you and her, I'll come home as much as possible."

"I'll be alright, son. I am the happiest when I am with my family, and you are here in my heart, always."

"The first thing I am doing in Nashville, I am going to find a nice place with a room just for you to come and spend time with me whenever you want, Mom. And I'll take you to the church, we'll share that experience together."

"Oh, I'll love that, Nicky!"

We embraced, a long warm embrace. My son, my soul mate!

As Suzy was still working remotely, I invited her to stay with us until Russell's return. Or if she would prefer, I would divide my time between her and Nicky. It was my goal not to leave her alone.

"Thank you, Mom, I'll be busy here, and I'll try helping you research and finding actual true reports and updates about what is being done throughout our nation and the world.

I see your devotion to this issue, Mom, and I admire your persistence on your quest for truth. Like you, I also love our country."

Every morning I pray *Psalm 91* – for both my son and my daughter. Now under these new circumstances Suzy needs more than prayers, she needs our full support. She is not alone!

'For God shall give His angels charge over you, to keep you in all your ways.'

During the first weeks after Russell left, she remained optimistic. They were in contact daily. Every day at 6:00 am she would wake up for his calls and they would talk at least for one hour. He updated her with information that sounded so absurd to us, showed pictures of citizens' arrests, of 'the wellness camps' that looked pretty much like concentration camps. It was shocking to see all of that.

Russell described to Suzy his 'underground' activities and efforts as part of the resistance to change the course of the mandates. He and many others were under pressure, and the more he became involved the more ingrained he was in the cause.

At times he spoke in code about an investigation on how the virus had spread to the world, at the same time, to more than 180 countries!!!

Suzy showed some concern.

"I am afraid for Russell, he is obsessed with finding things that he says are secretly hidden…"

"I know, Suzy, there are people right here in our country that think the same way. I don't follow them. There are other things that need to be done immediately to bring relief to the people."

In their conversations, Russell assured her he loved her and missed her terribly, but he needed to fulfill his duty as a citizen and a human being, helping his countrymen and his family.

Suzy was understanding and patient, and also hopeful that by the end of his sabbatical in mid-January he would be back to resume their lives. She temporarily discontinued the search for a house, waiting for his return.

Thanksgiving came around, only the three of us, it was not much of a celebration, but we counted our blessings and hoped that better days were about to come to all.

It was a sad time, I remembered Rebekah, it had been a year since she left…

There were developments in my daughter's company that made her very excited. A date was set for them to occupy the new building in Potomac, where they would be working in the office again, like old times.

Her employer, pleased with her long-term efficiency and dedication, and her willingness to relocate residence to be close to work, awarded her with a considerable promotion. Suzy was exultant!

"I am really thrilled. In the new building I will be head of a new department, a new area for online publications, including a new staff. I love my job and my company, this is all so rewarding!"

"Things are looking up, Suzy, well deserved, I am happy for you. Are you telling this to Russell?"

"I told Russell, and I am waiting for his return to look for our house, I definitely need to be close to the office in the spring."

Although Suzy showed optimism, many times I saw her crying. But she dried her tears and continued on. "I miss Russell…"

Anyway, with much hope we celebrated Christmas and my son's birthday. He was only twelve when we moved here, it has been twenty years, the most transformative years of our lives.

Suzy was anxious, Russell did not confirm his flight back, he needed to be back at work on January 15th. We couldn't understand why he was taking his time.

I tried to shake up my feelings about it and not bring more worry into Suzy's mind. I had a feeling something was not right. I prayed and prayed for clarity, *'Oh, Lord, Thy will be done...'*

At the year's end we were tired, it was a harsh year and not much had changed, at the contrary things only got worse worldwide, many were discouraged.

As 2022 started many of us renewed our commitment to continue standing, and decreed that justice, revelation and restoration will happen in our nation, and it will spread out into the world! Our hearts were filled with renewed hope!

'Now faith is the substance of things hoped for, the evidence of things not seen.'
Hebrews 11:1

I spent some quiet time reading speeches from some of our former Presidents and more recent ones, finding commonalities among them, endorsing the same sentiments regarding liberty and freedom. This just made me more resolved to continue my quest.

In his 1796 Farewell Address, George Washington warned his fellow countrymen:

'The habits of thinking in a free Country should prevail and that the division of powers between the different 'spheres of government should be jealously guarded.' He suspected that this would not be the case over time and that one branch of government would prevail over the others and that this would be' the customary weapon by which free governments are destroyed.'

From Abraham Lincoln:

'Let every American, every lover of liberty, every well-wisher to his posterity, swear by the blood of the Revolution, never to violate in the least particular, the laws of the country; and never to tolerate their violation by others.'

Nicky went to Nashville to finalize his business agreement with Jason, and also look for an apartment.

The next day after Suzy's early call with Russell, she locked herself in her room for the entire morning, sobbing, screaming at times.

I knocked and asked her to talk to me, I would only listen.

"I am here for you, Suzy! With all my heart!"

She took her time, then told me Russell had dropped a bomb!

In my wildest imagination I could not have anticipated it. He was not coming back, he was going to remain in Australia indefinitely, until he and the people he was associated with achieve their goals, which was to bring their country back on track.

'He couldn't leave that battle unfinished he couldn't abandon his family.'

He asked Suzy to come and join him, 'He loved her, he wanted her at his side fighting right along for his cause…'

My daughter was in distress.

"I am sorry, Suzy, very sorry. What are you going to do?"

"I don't know, Mom, I was so devastated and emotional, I couldn't respond. I need to cool my head and make the most sensible decision. All my life, my future, is at stake. We have been married for three years and I could never suspect he would propose anything like that. This is not what we have planned. I am thirty-five years old, ready to start a family, we were looking forward to our new home and a baby… All of a sudden, he wants me to uproot and change everything?"

"You are right about not making a rushed or an emotional decision, Suzy. Too much is at stake."

"I love Russell, Mom, I can't see my life without him, he is the one that I married for good, to build a family and to grow old together…"

186

"What is he doing with his job at NIH?"

"He quit it already! Without sharing anything with me, he now said 'the job was meaningless to him'..."

"So, he does not have a job waiting for him anymore. Yes, Suzy, it is shocking, and it is pretty serious, it looks like he has made a permanent decision."

"Mom, I need to be alone for a while to think this through. I am going back to my apartment, I will call you soon, I promise."

"I'll pray for you. Keep calm, sort your feelings out, above all just do what you always did, Suzy, listen to your heart and be true to yourself!"

Suzy left.

The next morning, I received a letter from the Homeowners Association with more unsettling news. They informed the residents that a decision was made and approved by the board members to expand and improve the garden area for leisure and entertainment, adding a gazebo, a barbecue grill and a concrete trail all around to be used by the children with their bicycles or roller blades. For that purpose the old sycamore tree would be removed.

My heart sank, I was devastated! They were going to cut my tree down and I couldn't do anything about it. Unthinkable!

That process would start in the spring, and the recreation area should be completed by July 4th!

Regarding the tree removal it would be an elaborate project that would take a large specialized crew and trucks with machinery including a crane, for the removal of the branches and trunk. They clarified that the roots would not be taken out, that would require deep excavation of the area.

In a further notice they would confirm the date of removal, for all the necessary measures to be taken, like moving parked cars and blocking the street.

For a moment I was scared. I felt like everything was falling apart, my son was moving to another state, and now the possibility that Suzy would leave the country...

More than ever, I needed a friend to talk to. I couldn't speak to Suzy, she had important life decisions to make, and I did not call Nicholas, he needed to be free of burden to accomplish what he went to do in Nashville.

I left the house and strolled around, reminiscing about the people that in the past lived here and served as inspiration for my tales.

How sad, does anyone around here feel the same way I feel about this place? I won't miss this neighborhood after I leave, except for 'my tree'...

It was a cold day but I spent time under the tree, now looking lifeless. I touched its bare trunk, the peeling bark. On the ground around, brown dried leaves, remnants from the fall, laid. It was not pretty at all.

It looked like the tree would never live again, but I am sure that next spring it should be alive, covered by green leaves... 'Would I be here to see it?'

Then, I thought, 'They can cut its branches, its voluminous trunk, but they will not destroy its roots. Never! The strong and deep roots will remain forever.' That was metaphoric, like the roots of our nation, they are unremovable and indestructible!

I found myself speaking in my thoughts, 'This tree, this bench is my most definite place that marks my friend's passage...'

I was telling Rebekah how things are now difficult, confusing, with my family, financial and health hardships for all, adding this devastating news. I almost heard her laughter and her voice:

'Fasten your seat belt, my friend, you haven't seen nothing yet! Things will get worse before they get better, but you will survive, you are as resilient as our sycamore tree...'

Really? Did I hear that? I smiled! Oh, Rebekah, always so spirited, she certainly would say something like that.

Eventually the memories created under this tree's shade will evanesce in the past. That was a turning point for me. Here I was alone...it was time to move away. I returned home.

Later Suzy called me to say she was coming home the next morning.

"Thank you, Mom, for giving me space. I can see things clearly. I am going to call Russell to tell him I am not coming to Australia, not now, not ever. I will not give up my life here, my career and my family because of his sudden interest that doesn't absolutely fit the vows we made to each other when we married.

But I love him, and I still want to be married to him, therefore I'll give him some time to reflect and act on his new ideology. If he wants to return and resume our marriage, I will wait for him, within a reasonable time.

No matter what is happening to the world right now, our lives and our plans will go on at the same time as we try our best to improve life's common challenges."

"Well said, Suzy. You are being true to yourself and still keeping the door open. Russell was very leveled headed before, I hope he will also see the true way.

And, I am sorry, I just heard some news that disturbed me, as a matter of fact I am very upset about. It's regarding the sycamore tree, they are going to cut it down!"

"I can't believe it, Mom, why?"

"The Association is expanding the recreation area this spring. They need all the space, and the tree, it's too old... I am heartbroken. That is a majestic, strong tree. It feels like murder, I can't even look at it!"

"Oh, Mom, I know how you feel. I think it's outrageous. Maybe there'll be a resolution... I am sorry, I know how important that tree is to you."

When Nicky returned, he told me he will be starting his new job in two weeks. He was very excited about his partnership with Jason and his father. But most of all, he said, starting a new life was what he mostly needed.

"A new me, creating a new path for my life!"

"It's inspiring to see your enthusiasm, Nicky. You deserve a new beginning, son."

"Mom, I don't know how life is going to be, and if I ever will form a personal emotional connection, but one thing I know for sure, I will not go back to my conflicting lifestyle."

"Truly?"

"Truly, Mom. I am standing on my own."

My heart was filled with hope, I don't want to see my son go through life alone, but I am happy for him finding who he really is.

I didn't work much on my blogs or publications the last days

Nicholas was with us, I was helping sort out everything he was taking along, but mostly spending precious time with my son. I knew I was going to miss him… Although it was bittersweet to see him going into his new life away from home, I was totally supportive of him.

In February, President's Day, just before Nicholas was leaving, I asked my son and daughter to come with me to DC.

"We haven't been there in so long, and I would love to visit my favorite monument with both of you, before Nicky moves away. Like old times."

They both immediately agreed, although those days were freezing cold.

The three of us went to the Lincoln Memorial. And we were surprised by the crowds. I held on to Nicky and Suzy, up to the Temple. Looking once again at the majestic statue, I told them:

"Children, here when I was a little girl, my father introduced me to Lincoln, I fell in love with him. He was and is my first love…"

They smiled. "We know, Mom, and just looking at the crowds we can say millions love him too."

I asked Nicholas to read out loud the engraved south chamber wall. I wanted to remember his voice resonating in my ears, like my father's voice in that same chamber, over half a century ago…

'…That we here highly resolve that these dead shall not have died in vain, that this nation under God shall have a new birth of freedom, and that government of the people, by the people, for the people shall not perish from the earth.'

In my memory, my father and my son's voices are one! We walked to the stairs and looked down below across the Mall, the Reflecting Pool up to the Capitol was enveloped by fog.

"This gives so much hope, that all these people gathered today, a gray, cold day, are here to honor this beloved President and what he stood for.

They are all lovers of freedom, fighting to overcome injustice. We are one people, one nation under God!

Nicky left and I didn't shed a tear in his presence. We said, 'see you soon.' He promised he would come to visit us shortly, and I also should plan to come to spend time with him.

Suzy has been quiet, pensive and sometimes melancholic. She continued speaking to Russell, but she didn't comment much about what they were discussing. My daughter needed time to reflect on her new reality, and I try not to interfere with her emotions at all, although I am pretty devastated by Russell's actions, I do not voice my opinion about him. I truly believe he was not committed to their marriage as she thinks he was.

I prayed for my daughter, she needed healing for her heart, and my love and support, not my personal opinion.

Getting to the end of February there were rumors of wars.

'And you will hear of wars and rumors of wars. See that you are not troubled; for all these things must come to pass, but the end is not yet.
For nation will rise against nation, and kingdom against kingdom. And there will be famines, pestilences, and earthquakes in various places.
All these are the beginning of sorrows.
Then they will deliver you up to tribulation and kill you, and you will be hated by all nations for My name's sake.
And then many will be offended, will betray one another, and will hate one another.
Then many false prophets will rise up and deceive many.
And because lawlessness will abound, the love of many will grow cold.
But he who endures to the end shall be saved.'
Matthew 24:6-13

Another blow hit the world, the 'winds of war,' scary times! The invasion of Ukraine by Russia! How horrible, communism is getting emboldened!

Again, the media, beset by secular and worldly propaganda, loudly post their narrative. Because of countless examples we should consider that things are not what they say or seemed to be.

I just want the facts! Suzy helped me find international

independent sources, some from the ground where this situation is unfolding, and we found videos that make us believe that no one here knows the real story, but something is coming out of this that is going to shock the world.

A shaking is taking place in many countries and governments…

The ones that need our attention and support at this troubled time are the innocent people on the ground. With that in mind Suzy and I spent very little time discussing the war and helped whatever way we could.

We joined a Christian network that was sending basic supplies and even airplanes to transport many out of Ukraine. That became our focus.

Suzy had a frank conversation with me.

"I have been quiet, trying to make the best decision for my present and my future. Since Russell left six months ago my life has been on hold, waiting for him to change his mind, resume our marriage and our plans, but I am not waiting anymore, and I am not asking him to come back. What will be will be!

I can't live here or in Silver Spring and spend hours daily commuting to work. The new building is ready next month, and I am looking forward to dedicating myself to my new position, working along with my team. I am looking forward to that interaction very much.

Mom, I don't want to leave you here alone, are you still up to move with me? This is what I am thinking: I want you to come and stay with me in my apartment while your house is on the market, we will invest more time together looking for our house in Bethesda."

"Yes, Suzy, just like our old plans. Do you want to start looking for a house now?"

"Immediately, Mom."

"Oh, Suzy, I appreciate that so much, especially now, I can't stay here and see what is about to happen to my tree. I can't wrap my head around that decision. It is so cruel, so unnecessary!"

"I agree! There is nothing we can do about it. But, regarding the new house I need to tell you, that it is going to be a little different than what we discussed before. I will be purchasing it alone, I can't count on Russell's income anymore, and besides he took half of the savings we had for the down payment, but I can afford a mortgage, mostly now that I am getting a considerable pay raise."

"I will pay for my part, of course. Suzy, did he tell you when he took the money?"

"No, Mom. I found out when I checked the bank statement. That's what made me believe that when he left last year he knew it was not only for three months. Deceiving, isn't it?"

"Oh darling, I am so sorry. It's worse than I thought..."

"Yes, and he continues insisting for me to come to Australia, he dares to say that the future of our marriage depends on me! I have news for him, on our next call I am going to inform him that I am looking for a house, as we both agreed for the duration of the three years we are married, I did not change my plan, he is the one who didn't honor his commitment to me. I am moving forward."

"I know this is painful for you, Suzy, but I admire your resolve and the way you are facing this reality. I stand with you, I wish I could ease your pain."

Suzy cried in my arms. We cried together.

I can't deny it, I was melancholic thinking of all the years of living here and being inspired by Sycamore Place.

I would be leaving a whole past behind but carrying with me the memories of my children growing up, my husband leaving, and my most uncommon friend Rebekah... Unforgettable experiences.

I had my loving daughter insisting to share my life with her.

"I thank you for including me in your life, that is what my heart desires, to be close to my family!"

"Bethesda is just at the other side of the Potomac River, Mom, you'll love it there!"

"I will love it!"

Nicholas called often. He was doing really well in Nashville. Jason's father accepted him in their business as if he were a family member. He was terribly excited about his work.

"Mom, creativity is pouring out of me, it is so rewarding!"

I rejoiced for my son, but I missed him dearly.

After Suzy talked to Russell about her decision, he was expectedly unsupportive and started calling less often.

Consequently, she decided she was not taking any of his belongings, furniture, books, clothes, everything he had left. She packed it all in a pod and sent it to storage.

"It will wait in storage until I decide the next step, or who knows, maybe he will have a sudden change of mind and will show up here..."

Just then I accepted an offer and sold my house.

Suzy had met with a realtor, Preston, and with him we were actively searching. After seeing a handful of houses we were disappointed. Suzy's budget for that area was not enough to afford a property to accommodate our plans.

Discussing with Preston, he told us of a house in our desirable area that had all the potential to be a two-family home, but it was kind of different, it was not the classic old brick colonial, it was a contemporary split level!

We were not excited but agreed in seeing it.

And there it was, sitting on a rectangular lot, built on all the extension of the lot. It looked enormous.

A few steps led up to the front door. The first floor was impressive, completely updated, with large windows bringing in natural light, a super modern kitchen, three bedrooms, two bathrooms and a living/dining area. From the living area there were stairs down to a den/recreation room. To the left side of the stairs there was an open space with a kitchenette, two rooms and full bathroom, to the right side, a door to a laundry area, A/C and storage.

There was much potential, I could envision building a wall separating the den from that space with a large French door, creating my own apartment. Oh, I loved the windows, the daylight coming through abundantly.

There were two independent entrances, one door from the garage into the den, and a glass sliding door opening to a beautiful but narrow backyard, with bushes planted all around. My eyes caught a pine tree, around eight feet tall, right across, near the back fence.

"What a beautiful tree, evergreen, everlasting...!"

The realtor said, "It's a slow growing species, it will take a few years to reach ten feet."

I asked him, "Do you know the history of the house, the family that lived here before?

"The Grahams, a very nice family. This house was built for them in the sixties, they raised five children here, but as adults they all moved away..."

Suzy and I couldn't contain our enthusiasm for the house, which was completely different from what we were looking for, but there was something about it that captivated us, the layout was perfect to create two separate living spaces.

"Suzy, that pine tree, is a sign! An Appeal to Heaven."

"What do you mean, Mom?"

"I will tell you later, let's talk business now."

We went with Preston to his office. The property price was above what we had estimated, but he suggested that we make an offer.

"By the way this is an estate sale, they are willing to consider any offers."

He took our financial information and verifying my upcoming sale in Virginia he agreed that I had plenty of funds to afford my portion. I stated at that point that I was not going to pay only for square footage, it was going to be a fifty-fifty deal. The names on the Deed would be Suzy's and mine.

Regarding Suzy, she qualified for a mortgage, but disclosing that her husband was out of the country and she did not know when he would return, Preston suggested she speak to their lawyer. The situation could get hairy, when her husband would return he could claim ownership.

She discussed it with the real estate lawyer, and he recommended that Suzy would sign a legal declaration stating her husband had no financial participation in that purchase, and therefore he had no rights to it.

"Do it, Suzy, you need to protect your investment. There was a time, when your father left, Rebekah told me to immediately obtain a statement and Power of Attorney from him giving me the rights to our property. I did it, and that gave me the freedom now."

Suzy agreed, the lawyer prepared the document, signed and

sealed it, and we also signed our offer.

Preston told us:

"Keep your fingers crossed, I will fight for you. I am going to make an appointment with the Executrix of the Graham Estate right now. I will call you as soon as I have an answer."

After two hours we left the office, exhausted. Suzy got us sushi on the way home.

I told her, "That is our house, Suzy! I appealed to heaven…"

"It will be so perfect, exactly where I want to be, only ten minutes away from my job. Mom, what is all that about 'An Appeal to Heaven'?"

"I will tell you when we get home while we munch our sushi. I am famished. What a day!"

"Here it is, the history of 'An Appeal to Heaven':

In the 17th century, John Locke, a brilliant English political philosopher, wrote the 'Second Treatise of Government' stating that human rights originated with God, not government:

'And where the body of the people or any single man is deprived of their right, or is under the exercise of a power without right, and have no appeal on earth, then they have a liberty to appeal to heaven…'

Locke's appeal to heaven was not about prayer, it was about direct political action. This concept became a fundamental belief in American society, and was even mentioned in the Declaration of Independence.

George Washington adopted the 'An Appeal to Heaven' phrase in America's cause for freedom from Britain's dominion. Having exhausted all peaceful possibilities of liberty, the colonists realized that their only option was through war. Britain's military power contrasted with the colonists' lack of resources, made the attempt to break free from British rule look impossible. Unless, they thought, Almighty God intervened.

'We will appeal to heaven!'

And a flag was born.

George Washington designed it with an evergreen tree.

Evergreens symbolize longevity, eternity or a lifelong commitment.

The pine tree flag, as it was known, soon was flying throughout the Colonies and adopted by the Massachusetts State Navy, it became a symbol of the colonists' unrelenting spirit of liberty.

Now a 250 year old flag has been reborn as a symbol of our nation's covenant with God, waving all over America."

'The propitious smiles of Heaven can never be expected on a nation that disregards the eternal rules of order and right, which Heaven itself has ordained.'
George Washington

It's a beautiful story, Mom. Will the 'everlasting tree' make you happy? Won't you miss your sycamore tree?"

"Sycamore tree shall be always my symbol of strength and resilience. But I have a feeling 'Everlasting' shall be our symbol of hope!"

Preston called us the next afternoon, our offer was accepted, they only expected that we rolled things really fast, the house had been vacant for a while.

"The Executrix was happy that a mother and daughter would be living in that home! That was exactly her mother's, Mrs. Graham's dream, that never came to fruition."

"Do you know what happened, Preston?"

"The five children, two girls and three boys, as soon as they went to college or right after, they all relocated to other states. The parents, Mrs. and Mr. Graham, remained alone until Mr. Graham passed away. Do not worry, nobody died in that house.

At that time her younger son, recently married, was contemplating returning to the area. That's when they did the entire remodel. Mrs. Graham had planned to live downstairs, but shortly before it happened, her son had a change of plans, and went elsewhere. Mrs. Graham got ill and died in a hospital two months later."

"What a sad story, five children and none of them could be close to their mother."

Suzy was excited about the house.

"Mom, if it were not for you, I couldn't afford it. Thank you! I could never own a place like that on my income alone."

I was happy too, I'll be a co-owner, I will be in my own home, not a borrowed space. Thank God for my daughter. My family!

I was still at Suzy's apartment in Silver Spring and told her I had to go home to make the last arrangements for furniture that was ready for donation, and also to transport our belongings to vacate the house. I needed to stay at least for two days. My daughter drove me to Sycamore Place.

On the last day I had a mission to accomplish. I left the house for an early morning walk, and one last time strolled around. I was melancholic reminiscing about the twenty-one years of being there, finding inspiration everywhere and in everyone.

I went to the end of the cul-de-sac and sat on a bench under my tree. Its branches that looked naked and lifeless for months were now dressed up for the spring, displaying the first signs of the season's revival. A new beginning that won't happen, which made that moment even more cruel. In less than two weeks the tree was going to be destroyed. It was like a life sentence...

I looked up:

'Majestic, powerful tree, you should live forever. You have been here long before us, before these houses were built around you, and you should remain after we are all gone...

For over a century you are standing strong! Your roots deep into the ground sustained you throughout storms and blizzards, and scorching hot summers.

Under your shade I spent countless times of reflection like this. I have learned much, I had heart to heart conversations, built friendships and trust.

Sycamore tree, my symbol of resilience and strength... Goodbye!'

I had a knot in my throat, and walked fast back to my house.

I didn't want anyone to see the tears streaming down my face. I was feeling a sense of loss, mourning for this living tree. 'What was my connection with it?'

Under this tree I realized how long I had mourned for past losses. Mourning was something I had done many times, going into a new life, leaving the old one behind, but this time I didn't want to mourn anymore. I will only carry the good memories, accept life as it is, and fill myself with hope.

It was here that I accept that people come and go but we will remain standing throughout sun and rain, darkness and light.

I had stood up through hardships, and in this place I found out I was not alone, souls around me were also looking for a connection. I am not like some that don't have the tools to do it, some of us never learn to understand or respect others and they become unreachable islands in the middle of the sea.

Letting aside my isolation, and becoming more aware of my surroundings, I received the gift of inspiration and created new stories, new people, figments of my imagination that brought out my most inner thoughts and beliefs in a written form.

In this place I matured to be who I am now. My life was transformed, my faith deepened, and I finally left the past behind and learned to live in the present.

I arrived at home, the house was half empty but filled with memories, and I spent the entire day into the evening writing about my children growing up, playing, laughing and sometimes arguing...

I never had been alone here, even in times when I was walking through the darkest hours, my faith carried me through, I held on to the hand of the Lord and prayed one of my favorites, *Psalm 28:7:*

> *'The Lord is my strength and my shield;*
> *My heart trusted in Him, and I am helped;*
> *Therefore my heart greatly rejoices,*
> *And with my song I will praise Him.'*

Our moving truck came in the afternoon. Suzy was already there to bring me back to her apartment. Together, we walked through our empty house for the last time...

As we were leaving, I looked back.

"I shall never return here, goodbye, Sycamore Place!"

"All set and done, Mom, you had so much to do lately... I didn't want to overwhelm you, but you should know that I made a final decision on my marriage.

The last time Russell and I spoke he called me 'selfish,' thinking only of myself, my job, my new house while the entire world is in disarray, and he is there working to improve the lives of the people being oppressed, suffering...

What he said didn't offend or even hurt me, at this point I expect any nonsense from him. I didn't defend myself, I just told him that all of his belongings are in storage, paid for six months. During this timeframe he should decide what to do with them, and if he prefers, I will send them C.O.D. to Australia.

I also told him that right now is a very good time to start our divorce proceedings."

Suzy was unemotional, I was surprised!

"Are you sure that is what you want, Suzy? How are you feeling about this decision?"

"I am alright, Mom, I have thought and reflected, then I had an epiphany: my marriage ended last year, the day he left prepared not to return. I am past the state of shock, this is my reality.

Russell is not the man I thought he was, he did reveal his true self, and he did it well! May he be happy saving his country and his family.

I am happy here with the work I am doing for my country with my family! So, God help us all."

"What did Russell say? Do you think this can cause a reaction and he will come back?"

"He didn't say anything, and did not call me back yet. Maybe I surprised him, he expected me to cry or plea. If he ever shows up here, which I doubt, he has to start over alone.

My trust in him is gone, I am truly done!"

"What if Russell doesn't agree with the divorce?"

"No problem, I already spoke to a lawyer, I will initiate the process here by myself, claiming abandonment."

"In a way, Suzy, I feel relieved, your life is defined now. You are on your company's executive team, moving into your new home, building a new life, you are courageous and free to find the one who deserves you!

May God bless you, my daughter!"

"What about you, Mom, when are you going to resume your writing? I would love to have another book published."

"Oh, yes, Suzy. As soon as we move, I will continue using my mornings like I have been doing for almost two years, joining my prayer group, researching and contributing persistently. I believe we will see the results of our work and our prayers in the right time!"

'To everything there is a season, a time for every purpose under heaven.'
Ecclesiastes 3:1

And, I have all planned to write a new story, in the afternoons into the evenings. It is a sort of back in time tale of a bond, a soul connection that defied life and death, time and distance. Something totally different than what I have written so far! Imagine, this idea came in a dream, I woke up reciting some words and immediately wrote them. Since then I am fantasizing about it...

For the next three weeks I worked intensively with the patriots and prayer groups. We were aware of changes happening in some states, of things being uncovered under the arduous work of many dedicated citizens from all walks of life, lawyers, and state representatives.

We saw parents being labeled 'domestic terrorists' when questioning their school districts about their children as young as kindergartners and first graders being indoctrinated in transgenderism, critical race theory, i.e. judging by skin color versus character.

I also learned about adolescents being instructed into making decisions about their gender, without parents' knowledge or consent. Are they trying to take away parental rights too?

As our leader and President Ronald Reagan said:

'You and I have a rendezvous with destiny. We will preserve for our children this, the last best hope of man on earth, or we will sentence them to take the first step into a thousand years of darkness. If we fail, at least let our children and our children's children say of us we justified our brief moment here. We did all that could be done.'

The media's narrative was misinforming the people, who consciously or unconsciously, were beset by secular and worldly propaganda. Real facts were hidden, voices continued to be silenced, cancelled, and peace among men continued to dwindle.

'And do not be conformed to this world, but be transformed by the renewing of your mind, that you may prove what is that good and acceptable and perfect will of God.'
Romans 12:2

Even so, many became hopeless, crushed by weariness and unbelief, they had forgotten that America is a free, God-given nation, and we must remember and protect the principles of the Declaration of Independence upon which we stand: equality, absolute rights, and liberty.

'We hold these Truths to be self-evident, that all men are created equal.'
'That they are endowed by their Creator with certain unalienable Rights, that among these are Life, Liberty and the Pursuit of Happiness...'
'That to secure these rights, Governments are instituted among Men, deriving their just Powers from the consent of the governed.'
'That whenever any Form of Government becomes destructive of these ends, it is the Right of the People to alter or to abolish it, and to institute new Government, laying its foundation on such principles and organizing its powers in such form, as to them shall seem most likely to effect their Safety and Happiness.'

Totally absorbed I hardly saw time go by, and the day came fast to conclude our deal and close on the Bethesda house.

We didn't move right away, by my request Preston had arranged a contractor to do the work I had planned. A few days later it was all done. I had my own apartment, separated from the den by a beautiful door. Perfect!

On our moving day in April, I was surprised by my son. He came to help and spend some time with us.

Nicholas and I speak all the time, he updates me on his new experience that is going wonderfully. His work is engaging and meaningful. He is happy and very comfortable in his apartment. So far he is not socializing outside the people at work. Regis, Jason's father, has been a great mentor, especially in the area of sound and special effects.

"Oh, my son is here. Moving in our new place, the three of us together. What a joy!"

We were very excited, the house seemed even better once the movers placed our furniture. Suzy and I went minimalistic, we got rid of many pieces and brought only what was new and meaningful to us.

Nicky loved our house and complimented us for the great purchase!

He gave me a miniature bell.

"The Liberty Bell, Mom, it's the national symbol of liberty and freedom. Look at the inscription."

'Proclaim liberty throughout all the land unto all the inhabitants thereof.'
Leviticus 25:10

"Oh, I love it, Nicky! Can you believe I never saw the original? Never went to Philadelphia."

Suzy came around.

"You should see the real one, Mom. During our school years you made all of our trips possible, you paid for everything and we just enjoyed. It is your time to go to Philadelphia. It's only two hours away. One of these next weekends we can go together. There are a few historic sites to visit. I am sure you'll love it."

"Thank you, Suzy, I would love to go with you!"

After everything was in place we decided to stop for the day, have something to eat, relax and talk.

"Tomorrow is another day, I will set up my office, cabinets, closets, drawers, little by little... But I was thinking that I would like all my pictures and paintings displayed on the den's side wall. What do you think, Suzy?"

"I think it is a great idea, I can also include some of mine, it's such a high wall. It will look like a gallery."

"Yes, it will be pretty. I am looking forward to it, I have two very special ones painted just for me... Nicky, could you please help us?"

"Of course! Tomorrow will be art display day."

We were tired and famished, Suzy ordered pizza. It felt like her college years, when she would invite me for pizza on Friday night. Sometimes it's great to relive the past...

We sat in Suzy's dining room, sipped a little wine, and I said:

"Let's celebrate, today is a new day of our new time!"

"Mom, we have been discussing at length your contribution to the national issues, and I admire your persistence. Are you going to pause to resume your writing?"

"No, Nicky, I won't, but starting on Monday, I am going to manage my time differently to write my new story.

Anyway, I'll keep myself informed and pray for our nation and our people until the end of my days. Overcoming what seems 'impossible odds' is our responsibility. I agree with Winston Churchill's statement during World War II:

'When great causes are on the move in the world... we learn that we are spirits and not animals, and that something is going on in space and time, which, whether like it or not, spells duty!'

"We have learned quite a lot during this time, haven't we, Mom? I became so ingrained in the process that I can't stop. Where I am now among other things, I see how affected the folks in the southern states are, in different manners.

For instance, the last governmental policy of open immigration, about two million have crossed the border so far. They came from all parts of the world, for them there are no requirements, no tests, vaccines or masks. It makes no sense!

These people have no jobs available to them, and many lack of qualifications. This is a humanitarian crisis, and also a matter of national security.

Cities are being overwhelmed by crime. Farmers see their land being invaded by the hundreds, and they can do nothing about it. American citizens are crying for law and order to be enforced, and they are not being heard. It's a disaster!"

"I know, Nicky, our loss of liberty and other policies that hindered the economy are crushing the people. We need leaders who stand first for Americans. But there is good news, there is a spiritual awakening bringing an understanding that we, 'the children of God,' have been given authority over the earth. In unity with the intercessors – the Ekklesia – holding on to the power of prayer, standing together, we will remain strong, and we may never forget our nation's covenant roots with God.

President Lincoln's words in 1861, endorsed by other contemporary great statesmen, are timely:

'... Patriotism, Christianity, and a firm reliance on God, who has never yet forsaken this favored land, are still competent to adjust, in the best way, all our present difficulty.'

The Earth is being shaken! We have already seen a plethora of evidence, and much more will be visible to all eyes. See *Hebrews 12:26-27:*

"Yet once more I shake not only the earth, but also heaven.' Now this, 'Yet once more,' indicates the removal of those things that are being shaken, as of things that are made, that the things which cannot be shaken may remain.'

These days are unraveling the truth about planned propaganda, humanistic education, lawless ideologies and systems, and nefarious efforts meant to control the people are all to be exposed. This is not new to humanity:

'For nothing is secret that will not be revealed, nor anything hidden that will not be known and come to light.'
Luke 8:17

We will see staggering and undeniable public displays of truth, culminating in reversals of policies. The secularist and globalist orchestrators of the 'New World Order' ideology will resist of course, but we should not be afraid, we the people will prevail. Righteous leaders will emerge, and it will cause changes also to come to other nations.

Freedom shall echo through the world!

We don't know when but it will happen in God's appointed time!

Therefore, strong we stand in faith and in tune to the sound of the Almighty. *Thy will be done on earth as it is in heaven!"*

"Mom, what a conviction! From where did you take all of this? Are you listening to prophets?"

"I have heard of them, but this is just the way I feel. It comes from my spirit, I believe from the core of my being that everything will be restored. America shall rise again!"

'Behold, the former things have come to pass, and new things I declare before they spring forth, I tell you of them.'
Isaiah 42:9

"I admire how you stand, Mom! You just said 'in tune to the sound'... It does make sense, recently Regis taught me about the 528 frequency that he adopts in his musical pieces. Have you heard of it?"

"No, Nicky. What is it?"

"The 528 hz Solfeggio Frequency resonates at the core of everything, connecting our heart, our spiritual nature, and the divine harmony.

This tuning has been used since ancient advanced civilizations by healers and priests to manifest miracles. 528 hz is largely applied in our modern world in musical tunes and sounds as a tool for healing, stress relief and meditations."

"Is it a musical sound?"

"Yes, everything in the universe vibrates at a frequency, it is like a sound wave. It is confirmed by NASA, in recordings from outer space. Science proves that 528 hz is so powerful that it can change DNA."

"Fascinating, Nicky! Do you think that something scientifically proven like this is to a skeptic the proof that we have a connection to God? And that we hear Him?"

"It might! There are several websites available, I will show you some, Mom. You can check them out."

"Oh my goodness, I am always learning something new from my children. I am so blessed!"

Suzy told us:

"Now more than ever I understand why things got to this point, we were oblivious, complacent, but now that reality woke us up, we just have to keep fighting. And, one thing I learned, we should continue living our lives the best way we can, while dedicating efforts and resources, and volunteering our passion for a common cause.

I was feeling a little guilty, being so enthusiastic about this new house, and my new position at work, but not anymore. Everyone else deserves to have the same quality of life."

"Of course, sister, it is true that we can only give what we have, if we don't love ourselves, we don't love anyone else…"

"Well said, Nicky!"

Seeing my son and daughter engaged in lively conversation I had a flashback, the three of us were together on a similar occasion when we moved to Northern Virginia. It was a new start for all of us!

They were teenagers then, and both excited about the neighborhood and the new schools. I was looking forward to start a new job, and also very optimistic about our family's future.

Here we are again, almost twenty-two years later, facing new beginnings, united and together! And no matter how things look now, I am confident.

The best is yet to come!

I thanked God for the most meaningful relationships of my life, and silently I made a wish:

'May light and love shine upon you, my little ones!'

"Suzy, Nicky, you both know how much I cherish you, but it has been a long day, I need to rest now. I know you are going to talk until..."

My son and daughter accompanied me to my apartment, and made many recommendations for being my first night in the new place.

"Please, do not worry about me, I am right here. I won't lock the door, come anytime you want. Just one more thing I will do before going to bed is to listen to my most favorite hymn, *'It is well, it is well with my soul...'*

See, 'old people' develop some habits, and we can't do without them. And, I will have a new one, every morning I will look outside at Everlasting, my tree of hope, and I will *Appeal to Heaven* for blessings and peace for our nation.

Goodnight, my loves!"

Suzy and Nicky laughed and kissed me.

"You are not old, you are spunky and full of life. We love you!

Goodnight, Mom!"

***

It is well with my soul

When peace, like a river, attendeth my way,
When sorrows like sea billows roll;
Whatever my lot, Thou hast taught me to say,
It is well, it is well with my soul.
It is well with my soul,
It is well, it is well with my soul.

Though satan should buffet, through trials should come,
Let this blest assurance control,
That Christ hath regarded my helpless estate,
And hath shed His own blood for my soul.
It is well with my soul,
It is well, it is well with my soul.

My sin, oh the bliss of this glorious thought!
My sin, not in part but the whole,
Is nailed to the cross, and I bear it no more,
Praise the Lord, praise the Lord, O my soul!
It is well with my soul,
It is well, it is well with my soul.

And Lord, haste the day when my faith shall be sight,
The clouds be rolled back as a scroll;
The trump shall resound, and the Lord shall descend,
Even so, it is well with my soul.
It is well with my soul,
It is well, it is well with my soul.

The Tabernacle Choir (2017-2018)
Music by Philip P. Bliss
Lyrics by Horatio G. Spafford (1873)

www.ingramcontent.com/pod-product-compliance
Lightning Source LLC
Chambersburg PA
CBHW032120170626
46808CB00006B/2023